KRISTY AND THE MIDDLE SCHOOL VANDAL

Another crash, another scream.

Mr Kingbridge jumped on to the stage without hesitation and yanked the curtain aside.

We gasped at the chaos that met our eyes.

The scenery from the last school play, which had been propped against the back wall, had been torn apart, some of it shredded. And the props—furniture, rugs, a bicycle and a ladder—had been tied together in the centre of the stage with the ropes used to move the backstage props around. Clearly visible in the middle of the stage floorboards, in front of the tied-up furniture, were the letters "MK" in green chalk, although a different shade from the green I'd seen on the toilet door.

Also available in the Babysitters Club Mysteries series:

Look out for:

KRISTY AND THE
MIDDLE SCHOOL VANDAL

Ann M. Martin

Hippo

The author gratefully acknowledges
Nola Thacker
for her help in
preparing this manuscript.

Scholastic Children's Books,
Commonwealth House, 1–19 New Oxford Street,
London, WC1A 1NU, UK
a division of Scholastic Ltd
London ~ New York ~ Toronto ~ Sydney ~ Auckland

First published in the US by Scholastic Inc., 1996
First published in the UK by Scholastic Ltd, 1997

Text Copyright © Ann M. Martin, 1996
THE BABY-SITTERS CLUB is a registered trademark of
Scholastic Inc.

ISBN 0 590 13559 7

All rights reserved

Typeset by Rowland Phototypesetting Ltd,
Bury St Edmunds, Suffolk
Printed by Cox & Wyman Ltd, Reading, Berks.

10 9 8 7 6 5 4 3 2 1

The right of Ann M. Martin to be identified as the author of this
work has been asserted by her in accordance with the Copyright,
Designs and Patents Act, 1988.

1st CHAPTER

June had not come too soon. (If I were a poet, I'd add something about the moon here, too, right?)

But a poet I'm not. The chairman of a small business, yes. A thirteen-year-old eighth-grader at Stoneybrook Middle School, yes. A big sports fan, true. The coach of a softball team for kids, also true. Not a poet, though. And there was no moon, yet. At least, not much of one. It was the first weekend in June, and the full moon was a couple of weeks away.

But maybe the moon did have something to do with the events that followed. A long time ago, some people believed that the full moon could make you crazy.

Of course that's not true. But some pretty unusual things did happen at SMS,

1

all in the time that the moon was getting fuller and fuller. . .

On that Sunday afternoon of the first weekend in June, though, I wasn't thinking about the moon or poetry. What was I thinking about? Final exams, and summer. It was time to make plans. Time to get organized. Summer was almost here, and I didn't want to be caught unprepared.

I'm a very organized person. Anyone who wanted to describe me, Kristy Thomas, would say, "She is *organized*. To the max." I consider this a compliment. I don't even mind being described as bossy, which is another adjective that's often applied to me. I like being in charge. That way, I'm sure everything gets done, and done the right way the first time. (In case you can't tell, I have very strong opinions about how things should be done—and organized!)

I also think that being bossy makes people forget that I am the shortest person in the eighth grade at SMS. Being short doesn't bother me (except that, sports-wise, it doesn't hurt to be on the taller side) but my parents and my two older brothers are not short, so I expect I'll grow. Meanwhile, since I'm outspoken and occasionally loud, people don't make the mistake of overlooking me.

2

My family is larger than your average family. I'm not talking about height or weight, I'm talking about numbers. I've always been in a larger-than-average family. My father walked out on us when my younger brother, David Michael (who is seven), was just a baby. That left my mother, David Michael, me, and my two older brothers Sam and Charlie (who are fifteen and seventeen now) in what you might politely call a rough spot. (Only I don't feel very polite when I think about it.) We lived in a little house on Bradford Court. Although times were hard, we became very close as a family. I really admire the way my mum hung in there, working hard, telling us the truth but preventing us from worrying. We all did our share to help keep things going smoothly. Gradually our situation improved.

Then Mum met Watson Brewer. And fell in love. And got married.

We moved to a mansion.

Amazing true story, right? Watson is a real live millionaire. So now we live in a huge place with a separate room for each of us, as well as rooms for Watson's two kids, Andrew (aged four) and Karen (aged seven) from his first marriage (they stay with us during alternate months); our adopted sister Emily Michelle, a toddler who was born in Vietnam; and our

3

maternal grandmother, Nannie, who came to help out when Emily Michelle arrived. Then there's our Bernese mountain dog puppy, Shannon; our bad-tempered cat, Boo-Boo; and assorted other pets (including goldfish and hamsters). There's even a ghost who has his own room on the second floor.

OK, maybe not a ghost. Karen believes that the spirit of one of her ancestors, Ben Brewer, lives up there. But then, Karen has a *very* vivid imagination.

You see? Big house, big family, big potential for disorganization and chaos if you're not willing to Speak Up and See That Things Get Done.

In the spirit of getting things done, I decided to put up the hammock in the back garden, and settle down for the afternoon. I would take my books out there, do some studying and make plans. I found the hammock and lugged it outside.

Nannie and Watson, who are both gardening fanatics, were already outside. They were looking at the Busy Lizzy, which filled a whole flowerbed in one corner. Nannie had on a big hat, and overalls that were liberally smeared with dirt and grass stains, especially around the knees. A pair of gardening gloves stuck out of one pocket. She was holding a gardening catalogue open and pointing to something on the page.

Watson, standing next to her, looked thoughtful. He was wearing a big hat, too, and ancient khaki trousers that were decorated in "early garden", just like Nannie's overalls. He was wearing his gloves, and he was leaning on a garden fork.

Emily Michelle, in a flowery sunhat and a tiny pair of overalls, was squatting next to a patch of earth, digging holes with the help of Shannon the puppy. This was, I knew, Emily Michelle's garden. She dug lots of holes in it, and pulled up everything that actually managed to grow there. Everyone has a different idea of what a garden should look like, I suppose.

Including Watson and Nannie. Nannie lifted her hand and pointed to another flowerbed, still buried under straw from the winter. Watson didn't seem to agree with whatever she'd said. He turned a page of the catalogue, nodded at it, and gestured towards the same patch of straw. Now it was Nannie's turn to look thoughtful.

Serious botanical decision taking place, I realized.

I grinned. They didn't even notice me.

Just as Sam and Charlie and David Michael had hardly noticed me when I'd gone to the garage to dig out the hammock. Three pairs of feet had been protruding from under Charlie's old banger of a car, looking like some human version of the three bears: big, middle and little. I said hello to the feet. Someone answered from under the car, a muffled "Hi, but don't talk to us unless it is an emergency" sort of sound.

I wrestled the hammock into place and settled down. I picked up my maths book, opened it, and sighed. I wished I was a maths whizz, like Stacey McGill, who is the treasurer of the BSC (that's Babysitters Club). But no such luck. It takes hard work for me to get good grades for maths.

Still, I wasn't the only one sweating over numbers that afternoon. Mum was in the study, doing some work she'd brought home from the office.

At least I could do my work outdoors.

I settled down.

Two seconds later, two of my friends, neighbours and fellow BSC members, Shannon Kilbourne and Abby Stevenson, walked into the garden.

"Oh, no!" I said in mock dismay. "I was *studying*."

"Yeah, right," said Abby. Abby can be rather abrupt sometimes. She's the newest member of the BSC. She and her twin sister Anna and their mum moved to Stoneybrook (which is in Connecticut, by the way) from Long Island not long ago. They live down the road.

Shannon lives opposite me. She goes to a private school, Stoneybrook Day, and has a pretty full schedule of after-school activities. I don't see her as much as I'd like to. So I was extra pleased to see her that afternoon, (excuses not to do home-work aside).

"I was going for a run," said Abby. "Then I saw Shannon, and we decided to go to the park. She's going to take Astrid, and we thought you might like to bring her daughter, Shannon."

If that sounds confusing, it isn't meant to be. Astrid is Shannon's Bernese moun-tain dog, who is a pedigree dog. She had puppies a while ago, not long after our collie, Louie, died. We were all very sad (and we still miss Louie—no dog in the world could replace him or erase his memory), and we weren't really sure we wanted one of Astrid's puppies when Shannon offered us one. But when we saw the puppy, how could we resist?

David Michael called the puppy Shannon, in honour of Shannon-our-neighbour-and-friend.

Nodding in the direction of Emily

Michelle and her canine gardener's helper, I said, "I think Shannon has other plans for the afternoon."

We all laughed.

I swung around sideways and Shannon and Abby scrunched themselves into the hammock on either side of me. We began to rock gently to and fro.

"Did you hear about Brad Simon?" asked Abby.

"There's more?" I asked.

"No—I mean, I just wondered if you had heard anything else. I thought you would if anybody had."

"Who's Brad Simon?" asked Shannon. "Is he brainy. Is he good looking?"

"No, and *no*," said Abby vehemently. She filled Shannon in on the details. Brad is an SMS student who'd recently been caught stealing the answers to tests (he'd had a student job in the office where the tests are copied) and selling them as "study guides".

Abby had unwittingly bought one, and had been suspended because of it before everything was straightened out. After that, Brad had been suspended. And now, just before the end of school, he'd been suspended again, this time for much longer. No one seemed to know what the story was, only that he was the second SMS student to receive a long suspension.

Troy Parker, another eighth-grader, was also on a long suspension.

"So what's going on?" asked Shannon, intrigued. "Sounds like a mystery."

Abby said, "Either that, or the teachers are just extra irritable, so they're quicker at recommending suspensions."

"You'd think that having the end of school around the corner would make them happy," observed Shannon.

I shook my head. "It's not that. It's next year's teachers' contract. Watson and Mum were talking about it last night at dinner. The teachers and the school board are still negotiating. Nobody can agree on salaries—or anything else, Watson said—and everybody is being stubborn."

"No contract, maybe a teachers' strike, maybe no school next year," said Abby. "Don't tell Claudia, though. We don't want to get her hopes up."

We all laughed. Claudia Kishi, who is the vice-chairman of the BSC, and in whose room we hold meetings, is Not Into School. She prefers art, junk food, Nancy Drew mysteries, and possibly even having her teeth filled, to going to school.

"They'll work something out," said Shannon.

"You know what else is getting on the teachers' nerves?" Abby remarked. "The Mischief Knights."

Shannon already knew about the Mischief Knights, a group of anonymous kids who liked playing pranks and leaving their mark in red chalk or red pencil. Pretty harmless stuff, such as rigging the school's loudspeaker system to play the national anthem at top speed, so that it sounded as if a lot of mice were squeaking it, or sending anonymous notes to Mary Anne and Logan in what looked like each other's handwriting. And why? All because, according to Cary Retlin—a new kid at SMS who is, I am pretty sure, one of the ringleaders of the MKs—"Complications make life more interesting." Oh, *really*.

"Cary Retlin. *There's* someone I'd like to catch," I said thoughtfully. The BSC members had been special targets of his from day one. He had broken into our lockers and swapped our books round, as well as sending us on wild goose (or penguin) chases when we'd tried to solve mysteries.

"What you need to do, Kristy, is catch Cary red-handed," Abby said. "Get it? Red chalk, red—"

Shannon and I groaned. "We get it!" I cried. "Stop her, Shannon, before she puns again."

"Are you calling me a punhead?" asked Abby.

I groaned a second time and pretended I was about to fall out of the hammock. Abby has a crazy sense of humour. She loves jokes, and she makes the absolute worst puns in the universe.

Then, Shannon stood up suddenly and dragged Abby to her feet. I almost fell out of the hammock for real.

"'Bye, Fearless Leader!" said Abby. (That's what she calls me sometimes. Also Madame Chairman and King Kristy. Abby can take it *and* dish it out. Luckily, so can I.)

"'Bye, Punhead! 'Bye, Shannon!" I said.

They waved and left.

I picked up my maths book with a sigh. Soon, I told myself, summer would be here and I could go to the park any time I wanted. I began studying, but before long I realized that I wasn't giving maths my full attention. I was more interested in some other problems that wouldn't add up. Such as what was going on at school. Mischief Knights on the rampage, teachers talking about strikes, students on mysterious suspensions. . .

I sensed trouble ahead at SMS.

2nd CHAPTER

Social studies. Now, there's a class with a mystery name. If you didn't know better, you'd think it would be about manners. How to dance. How to eat caviare or something.

But of course, it's not. Which is too bad, because there are some people at SMS who could definitely do with a course in manners. For instance Pete Black, who is captain of the eighth-grade class. Pete's manners *have* improved since he was elected, but he went through a bad bra-snapping stage not long ago. And Cokie Mason and Grace Blume, the Tweedledee and Tweedledum of bad manners, spoiled, rude, and always ready to be rotten. And Alan Gray, who is the most disgusting boy in our class. I once poured glue down his shirt in fifth grade. He was lucky that's all I did.

As I glanced absent-mindedly around the room that Monday morning, considering other candidates for a class in manners, my gaze fell on Cary Retlin. Not all of the above rude dudes are in my class, but Cary was definitely present and correct and looking not one bit like a Mischief Knight. He actually appeared to be paying attention.

Huh! I thought.

Then I felt the teacher's eyes on me and tried to look as interested as Cary. As a matter of fact, I do like social studies. We just happened to be studying a rather boring part.

The teacher didn't ask me any questions, but I concentrated on paying attention anyway. Paying attention in class, even during the boring parts, saves time when it comes to studying for tests later. The things teachers like to talk about are the things that usually turn up for tests. At least, that's my theory.

At last the bell rang. I slammed my book shut and shoved it into my bag. Maths next. My rucksack has lots of compartments, and I have a system for it. I put my homework in one of the outside compartments, my notebooks in order in another, and then add my books to a third

13

compartment as I need them during the day. I'd taken my maths book from my locker before social studies. So all I had to do was pull out my maths homework and. . .

And. . .

And *where* was my maths homework? I riffled through the pages in the outside "homework" compartment. I couldn't see it among the other homework assignments. But I was *sure* I had put it there, and I was almost dead certain it had been on top when I'd zipped that section up.

I was about to panic when I spotted something crumpled at the very back of the homework compartment. I pulled it out.

Crumpled. Not neat. But definitely my maths homework assignment.

I let out a sigh of relief and began to smooth it out on my desk. I froze, my hands flat on the paper.

There were the questions, all right. But where were the answers? The ones I had written in so carefully the night before?

Gone. Every single one. I jerked the paper up and held it close to my eyes in disbelief. I could see the faint pencil smudges where the answers had been.

Someone had erased them. But who? And how?

The "who" answered itself. In the

lower right-hand corner, in red pencil, were the letters "MK".

The mark of the Mischief Knights.

My head jerked up just as Cary lowered his to zip up his own bag and slide quickly out of his seat. He almost made it to the door. But I caught him.

"You did this, didn't you?" I demanded, stepping in front of him.

A couple of people looked at us curiously, but they kept going.

Cary looked down at the paper I was holding, then up at me.

"You erased the answers on my maths homework, didn't you?"

Cary smiled. He didn't answer.

"You think it's funny? It's not funny, Cary," I said sharply. "It's low. Despicable."

Cary arched one eyebrow.

"But why am I surprised?" I asked. "After all, you and your Mischief Knights are the ones who are always interfering in our BSC investigations. The only mystery is, that you haven't realized that nobody's impressed."

"Investigations," said Cary, rolling the word off his tongue mockingly. "Oh! Do you make citizens' arrests, too?"

"We solve mysteries," I snapped, "which is more than you've ever done."

15

"Really?" said Cary, arching his eyebrow again.

"Is there something wrong with your eyebrow?" I asked, pretending I'd just noticed. "Have you got a twitch or something?"

That got to him. He lowered his eyebrow and his cheeks reddened slightly. He said, "The Mischief Knights—whoever they may be—could probably solve any mystery they wanted to long before the BSC even had a clue. Personally, I know I could solve any mystery before you could say 'Sherlock Holmes'."

"Huh!" I said.

"Well then," answered Cary, hardly pausing for breath, "I hereby challenge you to a mystery."

That stopped me. I looked at Cary suspiciously. "Is this some kind of a joke?"

"No." Cary shook his head, keeping his eyebrow lowered. "This is the deal. I create a mystery. You and the babysitter detective squad solve it."

"What's in it for me? For the club?"

"I back down. No more jokes. No more, er, mischief." Cary grinned. "From me, anyway."

I wanted to punch him. But I restrained myself while I considered the idea.

I decided it wasn't a joke. I decided that

it was worth it. "It's a deal," I said. "Your mischief days are almost over."

I started to push past Cary, but he stopped me. "What about me? What if I win?"

Frowning, I paused.

"How about if I keep your watch?" Cary went on.

What a world-class weirdo! I thought, looking automatically at my watch.

Or where my watch should have been. It wasn't there. I actually turned my wrist over and looked up my sleeve before I realized what had happened.

Somehow, Cary had managed to take my watch. "Cary!" I shouted, but he had gone. I heard him laughing in the corridor, but by the time I got to the door, he was nowhere in sight.

First the homework, and now my watch. I was furious. I'd have to tell my teacher I'd forgotten my homework. As I was a good student and it hadn't happened before, it wouldn't be a huge problem, just a major pain and an embarrassment.

But how could I survive without my watch? I looked at it a million times a day. I am a person who is never late. My watch is the reason for that. It's also a fun watch, digital, with a stopwatch, an alarm and lap counters, as well as a light. And it told the date as well as the time.

Great! I thought angrily, stomping towards my next class. By the time I won my watch back from Cary, who knew what day and time it would be keeping? And with my luck, he'd probably set the alarm to go off in the middle of the night.

How had he taken my watch? How had he got my homework? He was the sneakiest person I had ever known. Also, I had to admit, one of the cleverest. Practical jokes might drive me wild (after all, it was a practical joke that had once caused Claudia to break her leg) but Cary's *were* pretty amazing sometimes. Hmmm.

I vowed then and there that I would solve whatever mystery Cary threw at me. Solve it, and flaunt it in his face. Make him pay. It wasn't just about the watch and the homework and all his other stupid jokes.

Cary Retlin had finally gone too far. This was war. And I was going to win.

I was still brooding about Cary and the Mischief Knights at the end of the day as I loaded my bag with the books and notebooks I'd need for homework that night. Brooding of this level is very absorbing. I didn't even realize Cary was standing next to me until he said, in a quiet, confident voice, "So, it's a deal."

I managed to close my locker calmly

(keeping a sharp eye on its contents and on Cary). I turned to face Cary.

"A mystery war?" I said coolly. "Yes, it's a deal."

"Good," said Cary. "I'll leave a trail of clues for you and the members of the BSC Police Department. The answer to Clue Number One will lead to Clue Number Two, and so on." He held up six fingers. "You have six school days, starting tomorrow morning, when you'll get the first clue." He raised two more fingers. "There will be eight clues."

"Piece of cake," I said. "The Mystery War is on."

3rd CHAPTER

I was in Claudia's director's chair, my visor on my head, my babysitting colleagues around me in Claudia's room. It was Monday afternoon, at 5:40 P.M. (assuming that Claudia's clock kept time as well as my missing watch did). We were all there (except for our associate members). We'd just paid our weekly subs, and had arranged two babysitting jobs. All was right with the world and the Babysitters Club.

What is the BSC? It is a business that *I* started. A very successful business based on a brilliant idea, and sustained by a lot of hard work. No bragging here, just facts.

It all started on the first Tuesday afternoon of seventh grade, as I listened to Mum dial number after number, trying to find a babysitter for David Michael on a day when I wasn't available. Suddenly it hit me. What if Mum could dial one number and reach several reliable baby-sitters all at once?

I rang my best friend, Mary Anne Spier, who lived next door to me at the time; we then called Claudia Kishi, another good friend who lived opposite (we'd all known each other since we were babies), and she called Stacey McGill, a new friend of hers who had just moved to Stoneybrook. I became the chairman of the BSC, Claudia became the vice-chairman, Mary Anne became the secretary, and Stacey became the treasurer. We decided to meet three days a week, on Mondays, Wednesdays and Fridays, from five-thirty till six, at Claudia's. (She has her own phone line, so we wouldn't tie up the phone for other people in her family.) We let clients know they could call us during those times to arrange babysitting jobs. Mary Anne wrote the jobs down in what became the club record book, a notebook with a calendar for our jobs (as well as a list of all our clients' names, addresses, and phone numbers, the rates they pay, and special information about their children, such as who is allergic to peanut butter, or afraid of cats).

Soon we had plenty of work and plenty of ways to spend the subs Stacey collected every Monday. We use our subs to pay my brother Charlie for petrol, because he drives Abby and me to Claudia's house for meetings (my new neighbourhood is a long way from Bradford Court), to help pay Claudia's phone bill every month, to buy new supplies for our Kid-Kits, and occasionally to pay for pizza parties.

What are Kid-Kits? I'm glad you asked. They are the BSC's secret weapon in the war against rainy days and general boredom. We take them to problem jobs, or just for a treat. Basically, they're boxes we've decorated and filled with puzzles, toys, books, stickers, puppets and whatever we think would be fun (Jessi's has an office theme, for example). Some of the stuff is old—our hand-me-downs, or things our brothers and sisters have outgrown—and some of it is new. But it's all new to the kids we sit for. And what kid doesn't love to play with another kid's stuff?

When business started to take off, Mary Anne asked Dawn Schafer, who was also new in Stoneybrook, to join us as alternate officer (the person who takes the place of any officer who can't come to a meeting). Mary Anne and Dawn had become friends, something I was not too happy with at the time, because I didn't want to be replaced as Mary Anne's best friend.

As it turned out, I wasn't. Mary Anne ended up having Dawn as a sister.

Are you ready for the short version of a long story? Here goes. Dawn and her mother and brother had moved to Stoneybrook from California (after the Schafers divorced), because Mrs Schafer had grown up here. She'd had a high-school sweetheart here, too: Mary Anne's father! As soon as they discovered that, Mary Anne and Dawn couldn't resist helping Mrs Schafer and Mr Spier to get reacquainted. (Mr Spier had been single since Mary Anne's mum died when we were babies.) The next thing we knew, Dawn's mum and Mary Anne's dad were walking down the aisle. So Mary Anne and her dad moved into the Schafers' house. Sadly, Dawn decided not long ago that she needed to move back to California, because she missed her father and her brother so much. (Jeff, Dawn's brother, never adjusted to Connecticut. He had moved back in with Mr Schafer even before the wedding.)

We miss Dawn a lot. (She misses us, too, although she has her own babysitters club out there, the We ♥ Kids Club.) Dawn, who is tall and thin and has almost white blonde hair, was the conscience of the BSC, in a way. She is very environmentally aware, which has made all of us

23

much more careful about recycling and things like that. She never eats red meat and actually likes things such as sprouts and tofu (which aren't so bad, I admit). And her calm, easygoing nature makes her a great babysitter—as well as a good friend to all of us, especially Mary Anne.

Mary Anne and Dawn stay in touch, of course, and Dawn has come to visit once or twice. We call her our honorary member. But it isn't the same.

Anyway, after Dawn left, Shannon, one of our associate members (Logan Bruno, Mary Anne's boyfriend, is our other associate member—more about him later) took Dawn's place as alternate officer.

This did not work, because Shannon, although super-organized, is also super-busy. She just couldn't make it to all the meetings, and she couldn't take that many babysitting jobs.

And our junior officers, Mallory Pike and Jessica Ramsey, couldn't do it either. For one thing, they are called junior officers because they are eleven and in the sixth grade. They aren't allowed to baby-sit at night unless they are looking after their own brothers and sisters.

Luckily, Abby and Anna Stevenson moved in next door to me. We invited both Abby and Anna to join the BSC, but only Abby accepted (Anna, a serious violinist, wanted to concentrate on her music). So Abby became the newest alternate officer and BSC member.

Apart from the fact that we are terrific babysitters, we're a very diverse group of people, as you already might have guessed. But that's also what makes us so good—our unique combination of talents, skills and experiences, as well as our excellent teamwork. Our new business these days comes by word of mouth, from our regular clients. We hardly ever have to put up posters in the newsagent's any more.

"Any new business?" I asked, surveying my fellow BSC members.

No new business.

"Any new mysteries?" I asked, only half-joking.

Claudia sighed. "School?" she said, half-joking.

Or maybe she was serious, even though she was smiling.

Why would Claudia Kishi, creative genius and vice-chairman of the BSC, call school a mystery?

Because for Claudia, it is. She's naturally gifted at art, but most of the other subjects do not bend to Claudia's rules of creativity. Such as spelling. To Claudia, the alphabet consists of twenty-six letters that are meant to be arranged in as many different ways as possible. Naturally, her teachers don't agree.

Neither do Claud's parents, especially since Claudia's older sister Janine is a real, live, tested-and-proven genius who gets top grades and goes to college classes, even though she is still at high school.

Claudia demonstrates her creativity everywhere. She is one of the coolest dressers around, and she's always creating amazing outfits. They'd probably look weird on some people, but on Claudia, with her long black hair, dark eyes and creamy skin, every look is a great one. Today she was wearing pink jellies, white ankle socks with pink hearts around the edges, and extra-baggy white dungarees, cut off just below the knee, over a tie-dyed pink, green and yellow T-shirt with the sleeves rolled up. She had a ring on every finger and one on each thumb, including a heart-shaped mood ring, a ring with a little bell on it, a ring that looked like a cat winding around her finger, a baby ring with her birth-stone in it, and a ring she'd made herself out of clay and beads. Her hair was pulled back into three plaits, which were tied together at the bottom with a pink and green ribbon. She had on her peace-symbol earrings, too, and a badge that said, "Jerry Garcia Lives" in black script against a tie-dyed background that matched her T-shirt. She'd made the badge herself in art class.

Claudia went over to her bookcase and removed several books with gold and silver award emblems on their covers. These were books her mother, the head librarian at the Stoneybrook Public Library, had urged Claudia to read. Claudia had read—and liked—some of them, but her favourites were the books hidden behind the award-winners: Nancy Drews. And behind the Nancy Drews were what Claudia Kishi was now after: junk food. In this case, jelly babies. She handed these around to us, then reached behind her chest of drawers and opened a bag of pretzels, which she gave to her best friend, Stacey McGill.

Claud's parents don't want her to eat sweets, but she hides them in her room and eats them anyway. Stacey can't do that. She's diabetic. She has to watch what she eats very, very carefully, monitor her blood sugar constantly, and even give herself insulin injections every day. But while she and Claudia don't have junk food or schoolwork in common (Stacey is a maths whizz and she does very well in her other subjects, too), they do share a passion for fashion. Stacey, an only child who grew up in New York City and now lives here with her divorced mum, is seriously into fashion. She loves shopping, and she and Claudia can spend hours discussing their favourite colours and what they are going to wear to school the next day. But while Claudia's look is wildly original, Stacey's is more New York sophisticated.

Stacey is tall and thin and blonde, with blue eyes and dark eyelashes. One of Stacey's favourite colours is black—a New York City thing, I suppose—and today she was wearing black leggings, side-zipped flat black ankle boots with pointed toes, a silver-threaded T-shirt dress that stopped at mid-thigh, and heart earrings. Her fluffy blonde hair was pulled back with a twisted black and silver headband. Her outfit looked extremely well coordinated, and she looked a bit more, well, mature and sophisticated than the rest of us, which is more or less true, most of the time.

My best friend, Mary Anne Spier, is the secretary of the BSC. Like me, Mary Anne is short (although not as short as I am!). She has brown hair and brown eyes. And like me, she can be stubborn. But unlike me, she is very quiet, sensitive and shy. Mary Anne is an only child. Worried that he might do something wrong as a single parent, her dad was extra-careful and extra-strict. He even chose the clothes Mary Anne wore till recently, when (with the help of the BSC) she persuaded him that she was growing up and could handle a little more responsibility.

Now Mary Anne does her own shopping. (She has a sort of relaxed, casual look. Personally, I prefer jeans, a T-shirt or poloneck and trainers, a combination which some unenlightened people refer to as my "uniform". But if I had to shop and all that stuff, I'd shop for clothes like Mary Anne's.

Mary Anne was the first person in the BSC to have a steady boyfriend: Logan Bruno, one of our associate members.

Mary Anne never lets her relationship with Logan interfere with BSC business, though. She's very organized. As keeper of the BSC record book, she has never *ever* made a mistake. She's a terrific friend, too. Her sensitivity makes her a good listener. She doesn't speak without thinking, as I often do. She knows how easily her own feelings get hurt, and she doesn't want to do that to other people.

Mallory and Jessi are another pair of best friends in the BSC. Like Mary Anne and me, or Stacey and Claud, they have their similarities and their differences. Both of them like horse stories, particularly stories by Marguerite Henry. Both

29

of them are talented, and have already decided what they want to do with their lives.

Mallory's talents are writing and drawing. She wants to be a children's book writer one day. Mallory works on her writing all the time. She's even had a job helping an author who lives here in Stoneybrook, *and* she's won an award for her work. Mallory's the one who is more or less in charge of the BSC mystery notebook, keeping it up to date and so on. (We started the mystery notebook not long ago to help us keep track of clues and suspects whenever a mystery comes our way.)

Jessi's talent is dancing. She's won parts in ballets such as *The Nutcracker* and *Coppélia*—she's really good. Jessi goes to special ballet classes after school two days a week, and gets up every morning at 5:29 to practise on the barre her dad installed for her in their basement.

Mallory is also the oldest of eight siblings, including brothers who are triplets. She has brownish-red hair, pale skin and freckles and wears glasses. Mallory's medium in height and build, has been known to carry her father's old briefcase instead of a rucksack, and is a casual dresser, like me.

Jessi, on the other hand, has the lean and graceful look of a ballet dancer. She often wears her black hair pulled back in a dancer's bun, and uses leotards as a fashion basic. She has brown skin and dark brown eyes.

Like Mal, Jessi is the oldest kid in her family, but she only has one younger sister and a sweet little baby brother whom everyone calls Squirt. And like me, Jessi has a relative who lives with her family and helps keep things organized—her Aunt Cecelia.

Abby is probably the most independent of all of us. Mrs Stevenson spends long hours at her office, and travelling to and from Manhattan. So Abby and Anna make up a lot of their own rules as they go along. (When the twins were nine, their father was killed in a car accident. Abby doesn't talk much about that.)

Abby has shoulder-length, thick, very curly dark brown hair, and brown eyes that are almost black. She's medium height. She wears glasses sometimes, or contact lenses, depending on her mood. While she is comfortable in joggers and a sweatshirt, or ripped jeans and high-top trainers, I have seen her in more stylish clothes, too.

Abby also has severe allergies and asthma. As she puts it, "Life makes me sneeze." Life includes dogs, dust, cat litter, most dairy products, feather pillows, shellfish and tomatoes. Stress and the hay fever season make the allergies worse. Abby always carries an inhaler with her, in case she has a bad asthma or allergy attack. She once had a terrible asthma attack while babysitting and had to go to hospital, but she took it all in her stride. She doesn't like to talk seriously about any of this (though she jokes about it a lot), and she insists that she will outgrow her allergies.

Abby's a good friend to all of us, but not really best-friend close to anyone. She's a loner in some ways. But she is outgoing and very sure of herself. She's keen on sport and a real soccer fanatic. She helps me with the Krushers, the little kids' softball team I coach, and she's good at it. We've had our share of clashes, though. Abby just won't back down, even when I know I'm right.

Shannon, the only member of the BSC who doesn't go to SMS, is an eighth-grader at Stoneybrook Day School. She's an associate member of the BSC, which means that she doesn't have to come to meetings, and only takes overflow jobs that the regular members can't fit in. She has thick, curly blonde hair and high cheekbones. For school, she wears a uniform (which horrifies Claudia and Stacey, naturally), and out of school she dresses casually. Shannon takes school very seriously. She nearly always gets A's. And as I mentioned before, she is involved in an amazing number of after-school activities, from French Club to the debating team, which is ranked pretty high in our state. She's also the only eighth-grader in her school's astronomy club.

Our other associate member is Logan Bruno. Logan is a good-looking guy from Kentucky who, Mary Anne thinks, looks like her favourite film star, Cam Geary. I don't know about that, but I'll admit he's cute. He has brown hair and blue eyes, and he's not too tall. He's funny and good-natured, and although he's sporty, he has other interests. Logan is also a good babysitter as well as a talented athlete. He and Mary Anne are a well-matched pair.

During the post-subs collection lull, when the phone wasn't ringing, I told everyone about Cary's challenge and the Mystery War. "I accepted on behalf of the BSC," I said. I didn't expect anyone to say, "No way!" but my fellow members had every right to complain about me going ahead impulsively without including them in the decision. I rushed on. "He's going to give me the first clue tomorrow before school starts."

"We'll show him," said Abby, to my

relief. She and Jessi were sitting next to each other, doing stretches for their calf muscles. Everyone else nodded confidently.

Jessi said, "Clue? It sounds like a treasure hunt."

I said, "Treasure hunt? Did you say treasure hunt?"

"Uh-oh!" Claudia said gummily (she had a mouthful of jelly babies). "Watch out. It's that Kristy Has an Idea look."

"I do have a *great* idea," I announced.

"No!" cried Stacey in mock surprise.

I ignored them both. "Maria Kilbourne has been bouncing off the walls now that summer's coming. . ."

Abby interrupted, "What kid we baby-sit for hasn't been? It's only natural with the end of school almost here."

"Right. So, listen. Let's give them something to do that will help burn up a little energy! What about a scavenger hunt?"

"Or a treasure hunt," said Jessi.

"Or that. But I think a scavenger hunt would be easier. That way we wouldn't have to come up with a really super treasure. In a scavenger hunt, the kids will just have to find as many items as possible on the lists we give them. And we can organize the kids into teams to look for things."

"How is this different from my house, where I'm always trying to persuade certain brothers and sisters—I won't name names—to tell me where they've put my things?" demanded Mallory. But she was grinning. I could tell she liked the idea.

Everyone else did, too. In no time at all, we were having a BSC brainstorming session, flinging ideas around at top speed. Mary Anne, who was trying to write everything down, kept saying, "Wait, wait!" as she crossed things out and added new suggestions.

By the end of the meeting we'd decided to split up into three groups of two baby-sitters each. As the seventh person, I would be the judge. Each pair would choose one day to help a team of children search for items on the list. I would consider the items, and decide whether they were acceptable. After the third hunt, I would declare a winner.

"Now all we have to do is round up teams, and think of themes for the scavenger hunt," I said.

"School," suggested Mallory.

"Ugh!" groaned Claudia. "Art."

"Dance," said Jessi.

"Famous writers," said Mallory.

"What about summer?" Abby asked. "Or sport?"

I held up my wrist, remembered that

35

I didn't have my watch, then pointed to Claudia's clock. "Time," I said. "This meeting of the BSC is now adjourned. At the next meeting, when we have an idea of which kids want to play, we'll choose our themes."

"Not," said Claudia firmly, "school."

4th CHAPTER

Cary was wearing my watch when I saw him at school the next morning—my watch *and* his watch, both on the same arm. It was a look Claudia might sport, I thought wryly. I pretended not to notice. I wasn't going to give Cary the satisfaction of knowing that he was getting to me. But it made my resolve to beat him at this game of his even stronger.

Cary grinned his smug grin and handed me a folded piece of paper. I unfolded it. It said:

Get your Mother
(understands).

I stared at the paper. I looked up at Cary. This was not what I had expected. "You call this a clue?" I asked.

He grinned again. His grin was doubly smug now.

"This isn't a clue," I persisted. "Why don't you explain what it really is?"

"It's a clue all right," said Cary. "All you have to do is look beyond the obvious."

He walked away. I felt clueless, in spite of the piece of paper in my hand.

"Hey, Cary!" I called after him.

He turned. "It's simple really, Kristy. Even for you—"

"I've heard Mr Kingbridge has caught on to the Mischief Knights. He knows who you are. And if the vice principal knows who you are. . ."

If I'd expected that to upset Cary, I was disappointed. Cary just smiled again, and answered, "Has he really? How interesting." Then he disappeared into the crowd of students surging down the corridors.

I battled the tide, and found Mary Anne at her locker. She and I started speaking at the same time.

"Did Cary give you a clue?" she asked.

"Where is everybody?" I asked.

I held up the piece of paper, in answer to Mary Anne's question. Mary Anne replied, "I think they're all still out on the front steps. You know Claudia. She doesn't think she should have to go into school till the last minute." I nodded, grabbed Mary Anne's arm and dragged her out to the steps. Sure enough, Claudia, Stacey, Jessi, Mal and Abby were there.

"Get Your Mother?" Mary Anne read aloud. "What does that mean?"

"It's the clue. Huh!" I said.

"That's the clue?" asked Abby. "Let me see."

We passed the clue around. No one could make sense of it.

"Maybe it's half a sentence," suggested Mallory. "Maybe you have to get your mother to *do* something?"

"Maybe."

"I wonder if we should phone our mums," said Claudia. She paused. "But if I phone my mum from school, she'll think I'm in trouble or something."

"So will mine," said Stacey.

"I'm not phoning my mum at work," said Abby firmly. "Especially not all the way in New York."

"Maybe it has something to do with telephones," said Jessi. "You know, you think about calling someone, you think about phones."

"That could be it," I said. "Telephones. School phones! Pay phones."

The warning bell rang.

Claudia groaned.

I said, "Listen. Everybody investigate

the pay phones. See if you notice anything strange. We'll meet again at lunch. . . except you two."

As Mal and Jessi are in sixth grade, they have a different lunch period. Mal said, "I'll grab someone and pass on anything I find out."

"Me, too," agreed Jessi.

We split up and went to our tutor rooms. I spent the rest of the morning thinking about the clue. When I eventually had a chance to look at the pay phones, I didn't exactly feel enlightened. Except for the usual graffiti scratched into the metal, and the general battered appearance, I couldn't find anything that looked like a clue. I was holding a handful of change, contemplating calling my mum, when I heard about graffiti of a different kind, scratched into a different kind of metal—the cars in the teachers' car park.

Actually, I overheard the news. Cokie Mason, the Queen of Mean, was walking past with a group of kids. She was screeching at the top of her lungs, in a pleased sort of way (of course, Cokie would be pleased at bad news), "Can you *believe* it? I mean, to scratch *that* on someone's car!"

Someone else said, "I don't get it, though. Why would someone write 'The deputie head has no control' and 'The teachers have no control' on a teachers' car?"

"Because the teachers are losing it?" suggested Cokie's sidekick and yes-woman, Grace Blume.

They were all so engrossed in their gossip that they didn't even see me. Still, just to be safe, I picked up the telephone receiver and held it to one ear, as a sort of camouflage, while I eavesdropped with all my might.

Cokie gave a trill of laughter. (It sounded like a bird being strangled.) "That's not all. Whoever did it misspelled 'deputy' with an 'ie' instead of a 'y' at the end. Someone also wrote in chalk, 'Take that, Mr Kingbridge' in front of the car. *And they signed it MK.*"

"Who's MK?" asked Grace in a puzzled voice.

"The Mischief Knights! Who else?" snapped Cokie.

I nearly dropped the phone. The group drifted down the corridor on a tide of malicious delight.

The Mischief Knights had vandalized Mr Kingbridge's car? I couldn't believe it. That was a crime. Not even sneaky Cary Retlin would do that.

Then I remembered what I had told Cary that morning, that Mr Kingbridge was on to the MKs. "He knows who you are," I had said.

Had that driven Cary and company to go on their graffiti spree?

As the morning wore on, I heard more about what had happened. Of course, rumours are never accurate, but what it came down to was that someone *had* vandalized a car in the teachers' car park. It was a light green car, the same kind that the deputy headmaster drives, but not the same colour. Someone had made a mistake. Whoever had scrawled the graffiti on the car had wanted to make sure it was permanent. They'd written most of it in permanent marker, and had also scratched the letters "MK" into the paint with something sharp, maybe a key.

We'd almost forgotten about Cary's clue by the time we met at lunch.

"I saw the car," Claudia announced as she put her tray down on the table. Naturally, none of us even needed to ask, "What car?"

"You did?" asked Abby. "Where? When?"

"Well, the art room looks out over the teachers' car park," said Claudia. "It was easy to spot, especially with that green marker all over it."

"Isn't that the wrong colour?" I asked,

remembering the pencil mark on my erased maths homework.

"What's wrong with green?" asked Claudia, giving me a funny look.

"The Mischief Knights," I said.

Stacey jumped in. "Their trademark is red. They would have written in red marker."

"Maybe they wanted to throw everyone off the scent," Claudia suggested. "I mean, this is a serious thing, not a joke."

Abby said slowly (for Abby), "From what I hear, whoever messed up the car did it during fourth period."

"Figures in motion," put in Claudia. Seeing the puzzled looks, she explained, "The fourth-period art class is working on drawing figures in motion. So for the past week, they've been going to the track, or the football field, or the gym to draw people doing sports."

"So no witnesses from the art room," said Stacey.

"What I was *trying* to say," Abby interrupted impatiently, "was that if the Mischief Knights are behind this, Cary wasn't involved. At least, not in person. He's in my fourth-period class." She paused, then added, "Although at one point he did leave to go to the toilet. But he'd have had to run even faster than I do to make it to the teachers' car park and back. We're only allowed five minutes to go to the toilet."

"If it's not Cary, then who is it?" demanded Claudia.

I said, "I think it is Cary. He's just out to confuse everybody, as usual."

"Clueless," said Stacey with a grin.

That made us all think of the enigmatic clue. Our telephone research had turned up nothing. We pondered other telephone possibilities (the phone in the head's office, cellular phones) and rejected them.

I unfolded the clue and smoothed it out on the table next to my tray. "Cary said to look beyond the obvious," I reminded everybody. "So maybe it doesn't have anything to do with mothers. Maybe there's another message here."

"It's not grammatically correct," observed Mary Anne. "I mean, the 'understands' part. It doesn't match the 'your'."

"Understands," I repeated "Un . . . der . . . stands . . . of course! That's it! Under stands. Under the stands. There's a clue under the stands."

"The stands?" Mary Anne sounded puzzled.

"Give me that." Abby grabbed the clue, them smacked her head. "Of course. Look at the first letter of each word."

"*Get Your Mother,*" said Stacey. "Gym!"

"Under the stands in the gym." I leaped to my feet, but it was too late. The final lunch bell was ringing.

Once again we agreed to meet, this time after school.

Under the stands.

In the gym.

With seven of us, including Mal and Jessi, I hoped that we would be able to find the clue pretty quickly, especially after I saw what under the stands looked like.

Gum city! Not on the floor. The cleaners kept that pretty clean. But generations of students had stuck chewing gum to the underside of the benches.

Ugh!

I didn't say anything, though. I didn't want anybody worrying about getting gum in their hair when we were supposed to be looking for clues.

We'd been scouting without success for about ten minutes when a couple of guys came into the gym to shoot some baskets. If they heard us under the benches, or thought there was anything strange about seven of their fellow students ducking in and out under the stands, they didn't say anything. They were totally absorbed in their game.

"Hey!" said Abby quietly. "I know I'm new here, but, that looks like Troy Parker—the guy who was suspended. For two weeks, was it?"

"Yep," I replied. It was true. One of the kids was Troy Parker.

"No one knows what he did yet?"

Claudia, who was nearby, joined us. "Nope. But if you ask me, he should be suspended for his fashion sense. I mean, a red belt with that outfit? Everything he wears seems to clash."

The others were gradually drifting towards us, empty-handed.

Mal said, "Whatever he was suspended for, it was something majorly bad. I mean, it has to be. Two weeks? That's just short of being expelled."

"Listen, everyone," I began. I was about to suggest that we all go back to work, keep looking for clues and stop standing around gossiping, when I saw it.

A neatly folded envelope.

I grabbed it. On the front were the words "A Clue."

Cary is *so* sarcastic.

I held up the envelope. "I've found it," I announced. "Now let's get out of here, and start solving this mystery."

5th
CHAPTER

"Let's see," said Jessi as soon as we were out of the gym.

"What does it say?" demanded Claudia.

I ripped open the envelope (carefully) and unfolded the plain white piece of paper inside. Everybody crowded around to read what looked like a poem in the middle of the page:

a drop pf golden sun
just short of failing
a skater's figure
not him, you see, but
(where does it all come from?)

"Oh, great!" Abby said in disgust. "So now he's a poet."

We walked slowly towards the door. A seventh-grade teacher passed us, stopped and said, "Don't forget to remind your parents about tonight's very important board of education meeting." She handed each of us a leaflet. We folded them up and stuffed them into pockets and rucksacks.

Then we went back to the clue.

As we reached the front steps, Jessi said, "*The Sound of Music!*"

"The film? The Broadway show? Or what you're hearing?" teased Claudia.

Jessi grinned. "The first two, I suppose, although I've only seen the film on video. But there's a song in it that has a line that goes, 'Ray, a drop of golden sun'."

"Right," said Stacey.

"That's it!" I cried. "Line by line. We have to take this stupid clue line by line."

We sat down on the front steps of the school and thought. And thought. Was the whole thing a musical clue? In the film, the song is to help people remember the notes in the musical scale: do, re, mi, fa, so, la, ti, do.

We tried spelling a word with the first letters of the musical scale, but "drmfsltd" didn't spell anything.

"Not even," Claudia said, grinning, "in *my* dictionary."

" 'A drop of golden sun.' If Dawn were

48

here, she'd say it had something to do with the beach," said Mary Anne.

But we decided that the beach didn't hold any clues.

Then Mallory said, "Maybe it does have to do with the sun, though. You know, like in the song a ray is a drop of golden sun. Ray equals sun. So the clue— or part of it—is ray."

We decided we liked that.

Stacey suggested that we think of each line as an equation. Each phrase equalled something else.

Claudia groaned. "Maths!"

"Short of failing. To fall short is to not complete something," Mallory said.

Claudia brightened. "Well I don't always completely fail. After all, a 'D' is not failing." Her voice trailed off and then she exclaimed, "That's it! 'D'! It equals a D."

"Excellent!" cried Abby.

"A plus," I agreed and wrote the letter "D" next to the second line of the clue.

"A skater's figure is usually compact," Jessi offered. "Muscular."

I shook my head. "Doesn't fit."

"Don't they have practice moves?" asked Mal. "Triple axels?"

"Yes! And practice figures. Like the figure eight. It's basic. A skater's figure is a figure 'eight'," Jessi said.

"Done," I said, writing, "eight" next to the third line.

We pondered the last line for a long time. I wasn't exactly ready to give up, but I was growing frustrated and impatient when Abby shouted, so loudly that I jumped, "Not him, but HER!"

"Hey!" I said, picking up my pencil.

"Not him, you see, but HER!" Claudia shouted back, and she and Abby high-fived.

"I see, I see."

"Write it down!" Mary Anne urged excitedly.

I wrote it down:

a drop of golden sun = ray
just short of failure = d
a skater's figure = 8
not him, you see, but = her

"Ray-d-eight-her," I said.

Mallory wrinkled her nose. "Radiate her? Ugh . . ."

"Ray D. ate her!" cried Abby. "Only, who *is* Ray D. And why did he eat her?"

Abby and her puns. I shook my head slowly. "No . . . radiator!" I exclaimed.

Mallory looked relieved.

We repeated "radiator" several times with satisfaction, telling each other how clever we were and how easy this was.

Then I said, "And where does it all come from?"

"Where do radiators come from?" Abby grinned. "Well, first a mummy radiator and a daddy radiator have to meet. . ."

I punched her in the shoulder.

"The boiler room," said Stacey. "That's where the heat for the radiator comes from."

"That's got to be it," I agreed. "But it's too late to go back into school."

"Too bad," said Claudia with obvious relief. "We'll just have to do it tomorrow morning."

Unlike Claudia, I was ready and willing to bolt back into the school and make my way to the boiler room. But it *was* too late. The next clue would have to wait till the following morning.

"Everybody who wants to help find the clue in the boiler room be here tomorrow *early*," I ordered. "We're going to win this Mystery War before it even begins!"

I was still thinking about the clues, and therefore more or less about Cary Retlin and the Mischief Knights, that evening. The topic was as good as any because I was sitting in the high school assembly hall while the members of the board of education were being introduced.

I'd decided to go along with Watson and Mum to the big meeting. Don't ask me why. It's not the way most kids would choose to spend an evening. But it interested me. I mean, here are all these adults making all these decisions about the education of the kids, and what do the kids get to say about it all?

Not much.

I think I wasn't the only student who felt that way. I could see some high school kids among the crowd, as well as a fair number of younger kids whose parents had brought them along. I also saw Mary Anne with her father, stepmother and Logan; Mal and Jessi with Jessi's family; and Abby and Anna by themselves, which I suppose meant that their mother hadn't got home from work yet. I thought she would probably join them later.

Proving that I was a brilliant detective and had guessed correctly, Abby and Anna sat down, carefully saving a seat between them.

I saw Mr and Mrs Kishi and Janine, but not Claudia. This did not surprise me. Claudia's idea of fun would *not* include a board of education meeting. Stacey wasn't there, either. I wondered whether they were doing homework together or shopping. I was pretty sure neither of them had babysitting jobs that night.

The introductions ended and Sarah Karush, the chairman of the BOE, stood up to talk. She looked calm and in control. I think that is important in a chairman. And when she spoke about her regret that the teacher-BOE negotiations had still not ended, she sounded sincere.

Another good quality in a chairman. Sincerity. Of course, lots of politicians are good at *seeming* sincere. But Miss Karush sounded as if she really meant what she said. I decided I believed her.

When Miss Karush had finished, she stepped aside for Raymond Oates. Mr Oates looked a bit like a cartoon politician: he had red cheeks and a red nose, a round stomach and perfectly combed hair. And he was not even-tempered, I could tell.

"I'm the chairman of the board's negotiating committee," he said aggressively, as if he expected someone to challenge him. Of course, no one did. "As the chairman"—another pause, another glare around the room—"I would be neglecting my duties if I didn't mention today's events at Stoneybrook Middle School. As many of you may not yet be aware, we had a nasty incident of car vandalism, in which a student, or students, wrote on a teacher's car in permanent marker and with a sharp object, and left a threatening

53

message in chalk in front of that teacher's car."

I frowned. I hadn't thought of the message as threatening. I'd been too busy being outraged by the stupid, senseless vandalism. And worrying that it was Cary Retlin who'd done it, prompted by my taunt that the vice-principal was on to him.

"Discipline," Mr Oates growled, pounding the lectern with one pudgy, white-knuckled fist. "The students are running amok. The teachers have lost control. We have to take back our schools, and that means a return to basics. Reading, writing, arithmetic. Homework. And DISCIPLINE."

Some of the crowd broke into applause.

Mr Oates smiled a thin little smile. Then he said, "Unless and until such acts of violent disrespect stop, until the teachers show that they are capable of disciplining the students in their charge, the board will not budge in its negotiating stance."

More applause as he sat down. However, I saw that the teachers were not applauding.

I was trying to think of whether I had seen any students at SMS running amok. I wasn't even sure of what someone running amok looked like.

Mr Zizmore, who was the teachers' representative, walked up to the lectern and Mr Oates stepped back, giving Mr Zizmore a challenging look. Sort of like a dog meeting another dog it wanted to fight, I decided.

Mr Zizmore didn't seem to notice. He smiled at everyone and waited for the noise to die down. His friendly smile and calm appearance gave no hint of what he was about to say, making his words doubly shocking. "I have a sad announcement to make. If a compromise cannot be reached within the next week, the teachers of Stoneybrook will be forced to strike. We—"

Mr Oates leaped up. "Then the school year will be prolonged! And it will be the teachers' fault."

Looking angry, Mr Zizmore said, "I disagree. As do the rest of the teachers."

I stopped listening for a moment to shudder deeply. *School prolonged.* It was too horrible to think about. A lot of plans would be ruined. The perfect days of summer would go by outside, and we'd be stuck inside.

Good thing Claudia wasn't there, I thought. She would have fainted.

From the murmur that was rising in the auditorium, I realized that I wasn't the only one unhappy with this announcement.

Several teachers, a few parents and every single member of the board of education managed to get their opinions in. Just before Miss Karush stood up to speak again, one of SMS's caretakers, Mr Milhaus, said a few words to the effect that the teachers and the board both seemed to have forgotten about the importance of a clean school, because they supported the idea of cuts for the cleaning staff. "Ach!" he said with his German accent, "a clean school is important. Students can't learn amid filth."

"I'm sure no one wants to see that happen," said Miss Karush, taking back the microphone at last. It took her several minutes longer to create order in the hall. Everyone was pretty steamed up.

I looked over my shoulder as the meeting ended and saw that Mrs Stevenson hadn't arrived. I signalled to Abby to ask if she and Anna wanted a lift home with us, and Abby nodded. I pointed towards the exit doors at the back and Abby nodded again. "Meet you outside," I said to Watson, and jumped up to zigzag through the crowds.

People were in no hurry to leave. And everyone seemed to be talking angrily, at the tops of their lungs. The atmosphere reminded me a little of the time that a group of parents had tried to censor a Thanksgiving play Claud's class had written for some third-graders at the elementary school.

I'd almost reached the exit when two voices behind me caught my attention. I recognized them: a high school teacher (and one-time BSC client), Mrs Martinez, and Miss Karush.

"Believe me, the teachers have my sympathy and support," Miss Karush said. "But the majority of the board is, I am afraid, behind Mr Oates."

"Mr Oates!" said Mrs Martinez indignantly, but in a tone as low as Miss Karush's. "What does he know! He's independently wealthy. He doesn't have to work for a living. He's just using this to make a name for himself. You know he's talking about standing for mayor."

"I know. And I think some of the other board members know that, too. Nobody likes to be used, and we're aware that Mr Oates could be using the board, rather than genuinely trying to help further the cause of education. But this act of vandalism has thrown everybody off balance."

"It's very unusual for something like this to happen," said Mrs Martinez. "He made it sound as if the school is completely out of control. Nothing could be further from the truth."

Miss Karush sighed. "I know. But unless the board can be made to see that, and Mr Oates can be proved wrong, I'm afraid we're looking at school in July."

6th CHAPTER

The next morning, travelling on the bus to school with Abby, I was out of my mind with impatience. What if the bus were late, and there wasn't time to check the boiler room? What if one of the school caretakers saw us and decided we were up to no good, and wouldn't let us look for the clue in the boiler room?

Come to think of it, even saying "The Clue in the Boiler Room" didn't sound real or believable. It sounded like one of Claudia's Nancy Drew mysteries.

"I like this," commented Abby. "I'm the calm one and you're the one who's over the top with worry."

I sank down in my seat. The bus was going more slowly than usual. I was convinced of that.

My next thought wasn't any more

optimistic. It wouldn't be surprising, I realized, for a school caretaker or a teacher to think we were up to no good, after yesterday's vandalism.

Abby and I had already talked about the disgusting possibility of school being extended into summer. And about how much we disliked Mr Oates (Abby kept calling him Mr Votes). On the journey home from the meeting the night before, I'd told Abby and Anna and Watson and Mum all about the conversation between the chairman of the school board and Mrs Martinez, the one I'd overheard as I left the building.

But in spite of my worries, the bus reached SMS in plenty of time for Abby and me to join the other BSC members, and for us to make a mad dash (in an innocent-looking way, of course) for the boiler room in the basement. And not a single person stopped us on our way there.

The boiler room was *not* a creepy, dark place filled with cobwebs. It was a bit dim and dusty, but otherwise neat and clean. The next clue, in a white envelope labelled "Le Clue", was pretty easy to find. It was wedged behind a pipe.

I unfolded the white paper and read aloud: "Toasted gloves or barbecued bats, anyone?"

"Well, I don't *think* he's talking about

school dinners," said Stacey after a minute.

"It's a baseball clue," I said, not very brilliantly. I looked at Abby, who as a fellow sports fan, knew something about baseball.

Abby shrugged. "A barbecue at a baseball game?"

"Who's doing that?" Claudia wondered.

"There aren't any baseball games this week," said Mary Anne. "At least, not at SMS, so the clue can't be at a baseball game because you only have six school days to work this out, five now, so. . ."

"So it wouldn't be fair if we had to wait till after time runs out to find the next clue." I nodded. Then I froze. Barbecued bats. I had a sudden vision of the athletics supply hut that had burned down not long ago, a sudden *unpleasant* vision. Because it was something I had sort of been involved in.

But how had Cary known about that? He couldn't have, I reassured myself. He wasn't at SMS when that had happened.

"I know where the next clue is," I said flatly. "He's talking about that supply hut that burned down, the one they've just finished rebuilding."

"Oh!" Abby said. "A supply hut burned down in the school grounds? I'm surprised Mr Votes didn't mention that last night, too."

Come to think of it, I was rather surprised myself. But then, the culprits had been caught, so maybe it wasn't all that surprising.

No one else said anything. They knew what had happened when the supply hut had burned down, and what my rôle had been. But Abby didn't.

I wasn't going to explain it to her. Maybe another day.

"I'll investigate the hut during PE," I said.

"I could do it," Abby offered. "I always finish my warm-up laps before anybody else, so I'll have plenty of time."

"No, I'll do it."

Again Abby shrugged, unruffled by my abrupt manner.

Mary Anne asked, a little anxiously, "Kristy, are you sure?"

"Sure," I said. "No problem." I made myself grin. "We'll have the next clue by lunch."

But before my PE class, before lunch and almost before tutor time was over, something happened that made me forget the Mystery War altogether for a little while.

The SMS vandal struck again. At first I thought it was just another fire drill.

Then, as we waited out in the car park, I noticed the teachers looking worried.

Then the fire engines arrived, and suddenly I felt scared, and weirdly excited. Was Stoneybrook Middle School on fire? Had everybody got out safely?

The BSC members drifted together like magnets to metal.

"No maths today," said Claudia happily.

I didn't answer. "Look," I said. "There's Troy Parker."

Abby said, "Oh, yeah. The suspended kid who did something really bad. What's he doing here?"

Stacey wrinkled her nose. "I don't know. But someone should tell him grunge is old news. Look at those jeans!"

"I like the jeans," said Claudia. "But the shirt has got to go—or at least, go with something else."

"Maybe he found it at a sale of fire-damaged goods," said Abby.

We all stared at her.

Abby has a weird sense of humour sometimes.

As usual, Abby didn't seem to notice. Instead she said, "Wow! There's Brad Simon, with some teacher. Who is she?"

We looked over at Brad, who was looking at his watch. "I've never seen that teacher before," I said, puzzled. "I don't think she *is* a teacher."

Jessi slipped through the crowd to join us. "Guess what," she said breathlessly. "I've just seen Mr Oates—" She looked at Abby and grinned. "No, Mr Votes, talking to Mr Kingbridge. Mr K. asked Mr Votes what he was doing at SMS, and Mr Votes started talking about teachers 'failing in their security duties by allowing this preposterous false alarm.'"

"Is it a false alarm?" asked Claudia. (I don't think she really wanted SMS to burn down, especially once she realized that we'd probably have to spend half the summer making up all the lost school days.)

As if in answer, the firemen emerged from the building and went back to their fire engines.

Jessi nodded. "And you know what else I heard? It was the Mischief Knights. They left a green MK in chalk by the fire alarm that was set off."

I gasped. "Cary! Was anybody in class with him when the alarm was pulled?"

No one was. He had no alibis, at least from us.

The teachers began rounding up the students to go back inside. I hardly noticed where I was when I got into line. I went up the stairs, thinking hard, and almost fell over a cleaner's mop and bucket by a wet spot in the hall. I actually walked right past the door of my classroom. The teacher had to call me back.

Embarrassing. Especially as I couldn't work it all out. But I was sure of one thing—Cary Retlin was behind it all.

Wasn't he?

"You!" I said, stopping outside the hut, where I'd gone just before lunch, as I hadn't been able to make it during PE.

Cary Retlin turned, an envelope in his hand. He almost looked surprised

"Kristy!"

Not only was he holding the envelope, he still had my watch on his wrist.

"What's wrong? Weren't you expecting us to work out the last clue so quickly?" I felt smug, certain that I was right.

Of course Cary didn't answer. He just looked down at the envelope and smiled.

I held out my hand.

"But then, you've had a busy morning, haven't you?" I went on, when he didn't give me the envelope straight away. "False alarms. Who knows what else, what other *vandalism*."

"You'd like that, wouldn't you?" Cary asked. "Don't forget to look beyond the obvious, Kristy."

That was good enough for me. If

someone accused me of something I didn't do, I'd tell them how wrong they were, loud and clear. The fact that Cary didn't deny a thing made me more certain than ever that he was guilty.

"I'm not surprised," I said. I thrust my hand, palm up, towards him again.

He laid the envelope on it. "Best of luck to you and the babysitting detectives," he said, making it sound like a challenge.

"Keep your luck!" I shot back. "You're going to need it."

I went over to the canteen.

By the time I'd put my tray on the table where everyone else was eating lunch, the warning bell was ringing.

"Did you get it?" asked Abby. I nodded, chewing rapidly, and patted my pocket. "Cary 'etlin's'erk," I said with my mouth full.

I swallowed. "He was still at the hut, holding the envelope. I don't think he expected us to solve the last clue so quickly."

"Huh!" Stacey scoffed.

"We're going to be late," said Mary Anne. "Maybe we should save the clue for the BSC meeting."

I nodded, continuing to chew.

I only just made it to my next class on time.

But not to worry. We'd hardly settled

66

in our seats when the fire alarm began to shriek.

Here we go again! I thought. I was right. It turned out to be another false alarm. The fire brigade appeared before the last of us made it outside. Just as quickly, they were gone.

Another alarm. Another MK signature in green chalk. And this time Cary, who had English with Stacey during that period, had not been in class, according to Stacey's between-class, mid-corridor debriefing with me.

Hmmm. . .

That afternoon, our bus was late.

"Have you ever noticed," said Abby, who was waiting for the bus with me, "that the bus is *always* on time or early on the way to school? It's only when you're trying to leave that the Wheeze Wagon goes off the track." (Abby calls our bus the Wheeze Wagon because it sounds like a car with asthma, she says.)

"True," agreed Stacey, who was standing with us. She was waiting for Mallory. They were on their way to the first BSC scavenger hunt.

"Do you think Cary did it? The Mischief Knights?" I asked abruptly.

Neither Abby nor Stacey had to ask what I meant.

"Those stunts could have pretty serious consequences," said Abby. "Would the MKs really go that far? Not that I know Cary all that well."

"I don't think anybody does," I said.

Stacey looked thoughtful. "I agree with Abby. I mean, what they did to the car, whoever did it, wasn't funny. It was really destructive."

I had to agree with that. Much as I didn't like Cary, I didn't see him sinking to actual vandalism. Cary was too sure of his own cleverness, and the vandalism wasn't very clever.

But it was hard to ignore those times when he didn't have an alibi. And the fact that he didn't deny being the culprit.

With a sigh, Abby said, "Well, whoever's doing it, I wish they'd stop. I mean, I don't mind missing a couple of classes for fire drills, but if I have to go to summer school to make up for lost days because the teachers go on strike, I'll go *spare*."

"It's the vandal's fault. If I didn't know better, I'd think Mr Oates-votes was doing it himself, to drum up support when he stands for mayor," said Stacey.

"He was there for the fire alarm," I reminded her. "Remember? Mr Kingbridge was surprised to see him."

"Yes, well, Troy Parker and Brad Simon were there too, for that matter. We know Brad Simon is a jerk, and we know Troy Parker was suspended for something serious," Abby pointed out.

"For that matter, Mal saw Mr Milhaus walking past her classroom door just before the alarm went off. And it was the alarm near her classroom that someone set off," I added.

Abby grinned. "Everybody's a suspect except you and me, and I'm not so sure about you."

"A pattern or motive. That's what we should be looking for," announced Stacey. She held up her fingers and counted off: "One: a damaged car with a threat to Mr Kingbridge; two: two false fire alarms; three: all three are signed MK, in green."

"Cars, false alarms and green chalk. I can't see a pattern there," I said. "Isn't there anything else?"

"They aren't good spellers," Stacey observed. "Isn't that what Cokie said? They misspelled deputy."

Just then Abby jumped up. (Abby never does anything slowly, or even at normal speed.) "There's our bus."

"See you lot later," said Stacey, and we went our separate ways till the BSC meeting.

7th
CHAPTER

wednesday

The first day of the scavenger hunt
reminded me of cleaning day at my house.
A herd of kids finding all kinds of things
and trying to figure out who they belong
to — and what they are!

But it was fun, Mal. You have to
admit it was fun. . . .

The scavenger hunt headquarters for the day was the Pike house, where Mal and Stacey met (or maybe it would be more accurate to say "were met by") seven Pikes, two Arnolds, two Braddocks and two Hills: thirteen scavengers in all.

They were careering around the Pike garden like pinballs. The minute Mal and Stacey appeared, the group converged on them. Stacey closed her eyes, half-expecting to be trampled by a herd of scavenger hunters. But Mal, who has slightly more experience with charging herds of kids, said in a loud, calm voice, "Everybody sit down. We can't start the hunt until everybody SITS DOWN."

She pointed to the grass in front of her. Stacey opened her eyes. The kids were sorting themselves out, and soon every one of them was sitting on the grass.

Mal nodded at Stacey.

Stacey nodded back and cleared her throat. "OK, you lot, does everybody know what a scavenger hunt is?"

Hands shot up. Kids wriggled. A few voices cried, "I know, I know!"

"Carolyn?" said Stacey. "Do you want to tell us?"

Carolyn Arnold stood up and said importantly, "A scavenger hunt is when you go hunting for things like a buzzard does. A buzzard is a scavenger, you know."

Considerably startled, Mal interrupted, "Well, yes, that's sort of where the name comes from. You hunt for all kinds of different things."

"But you don't eat them like a buzzard," interrupted Carolyn's twin sister Marilyn.

"UGH!" shrieked Margo Pike.

"Definitely not!" cried Stacey.

Waving her arms in the air, Haley Braddock jumped up. "It's where you have a list and you hunt for things on the list, right? You go around and ask people if they have what you're looking for."

Stacey nodded.

"And you do it in teams," Adam, one of the Pike triplets, added. "And the best team finds all the stuff on the list first and wins! Let's start now!"

He and the other triplets, Byron and Jordan, immediately leaped to their feet.

"NO!" said Mal.

Stacey explained, "We can't start until we're divided into teams and we can't divide into teams until everybody sits down again."

Once more everybody sat down.

Mal reached into her bag and said, "OK. We have two copies of the list of things we're looking for here, one copy for

72

each team. You earn points for finishing first."

"What if neither team finds everything on the list?" asked Nicky Pike.

"Then the team with the most things earns the points for winning."

Stacey and Mal went on to explain that the list was of clues, rather than specific items, and that several different items might fit a description on the list. For example, the clue might read, "Get a Life." One team might track down a *Life* magazine, while another might look for a box of Life breakfast cereal. Points would also be given for the most original item in any category. The theme we had chosen for the first hunt, in spite of Claudia's protests, was school. It was a big, easy category, with lots of possibilities. (Claudia had eventually given in, saying, "As long as it's not *my* scavenger hunt theme.")

"The people in each team have to stay together," Mal finished. "No dividing up to find different things on the list."

"Rats!" mumbled Byron.

"The objects can be found, or you can get them by asking people for them," said Stacey. "But you can't ask anybody for more than one thing on the list."

They divided into teams: Byron, Adam, Jordan, Carolyn, Haley, Norman Hill and

Claire Pike went with Mal. Stacey's team included Vanessa, Nicky, Margo, Marilyn, Matthew Braddock and Sarah Hill.

They were about to set off when Byron said suddenly, "We haven't got a team name."

Nicky said, "We want a name, too."

"Pikes' Losers," Byron teased, pointing at Vanessa, Nicky and Margo.

"Ha, ha!" said Margo. "We're going to find everything first and win. You'll be the losers."

"Finders keepers, losers weepers!" chanted Vanessa. Then she shouted, "That's it. Our team name is Finders Keepers!"

"That's a good one," said Stacey admiringly.

Jordan scowled. "Well, we're the Dream Team."

Vanessa smiled. "Go ahead. Dream on!"

"The Dream Team! I like it," said Mal hastily. "Let's coordinate watches."

Mal and Stacey coordinated watches.

"We'll meet back here in an hour," said Mal. "That means even if you haven't found everything on your list, you have to come back here. And if you are late, you lose points."

"Eat our dust!" shouted Adam (he'd

been watching a lot of bad films on video recently). The Dream Team took off.

"Losers weepers!" Margo shouted back.

Stacey handed Vanessa the piece of paper with the list of clues. Vanessa read the first clue aloud:

"For the beginning of the school caper, remember that this holds the paper," Vanessa read aloud. "Not a bad rhyme." She frowned. "But what holds the paper?"

"A newspaper stand?" said Marilyn.

Stacey signed "What holds paper?" to Matthew Braddock, who quickly signed something back. (Matthew is deaf and uses American Sign Language. All of us sitters have learned enough ASL to talk to him a bit.)

"A notebook," said Stacey. "That's a good idea, Matt."

"Or a paper clip," Nicky offered. "Paper clips hold paper."

Vanessa laughed. "I think we'd be in trouble if we tried to bring back a newspaper stand."

"Yes, but we'd get a *lot* of points for it," said Nicky.

"We'll ask for a notebook or a paper clip and let whoever is giving it to us choose," suggested Sarah.

Meanwhile, in the front garden, the

Pike triplets were arguing vigorously in favour of a tree branch as the answer to the first clue. "A tree, see?" Adam explained. "It's where paper comes from. Trees are used to make paper. Pine trees."

"Pine trees?" said Mal.

"Maybe," said Adam, undaunted.

"We can't knock on someone's door and ask for a tree," said Carolyn scornfully.

"But we can just pick a pine tree branch off the ground," argued Byron.

The triplets won. The first item was a tree branch, which Mal ended up carrying for most of the rest of the scavenger hunt.

By the time the hour was up, the kids had assembled an amazing assortment of school-related (and not so school-related) items from the clues given. The two groups met at the gate to the Pike's garden when the time was up.

"Nice tree," said Stacey, grinning at Mal.

"Whose trainers?" retorted Mal. The clue had been "Here's a transportation rule/This helps you make your way to school." Stacey's group had decided not on the bus (or bus tokens) or a picture of a bicycle, but on their feet. The trainers were supposed to represent feet.

"Did you find everything?" shouted Nicky. "We did!"

"We did, too," replied Haley.

Nicky looked crushed. "You did?"

"No," said Mal, "we didn't."

Haley grinned. Nicky stuck out his tongue.

It turned out that Stacey's group had scored one more item than Mal's team. But Mal's team had several things at least as original as the tree branch.

Everyone went home, except Mal and Stacey. Loading up the two teams' items in separate boxes, carefully labelled, they made their way to the BSC meeting with the loot.

8th CHAPTER

I was fascinated with the boxes of scavenger hunt items. "Shoes? A tree branch? What happened to, you know, bicycles and paper clips?"

Mal grinned. "They were going after the points for originality."

"This is great," Claudia said, kneeling next to me and peering into one of the boxes. "It makes me see school in a whole different light. Paper as trees in disguise ... I like that." Then Claud noticed something else. "Ugh! What's that?" she asked.

"That was Norman's contribution—under the 'lunch at school' category," Mal explained. "It's some leftovers from the Papadakises fridge, mixed together."

"We can throw it away," I said. "I'll remember it."

"Kristy, everybody's here. How about showing us the clue," said Abby impatiently.

How could I have forgotten? I'd been so excited by the scavenger hunt loot that I had almost forgotten the next clue in the Mystery War.

Quickly I sat down in the director's chair. And of course, the phone rang. And rang. It's a bit like washing your car to make it rain, I suppose. Anyway, we didn't get to the clue until four phone calls later.

But at last I was able to pull the envelope out. I held it up.

"Open it!" cried Mal impatiently.

"Before the phone rings again," added Jessi.

That inspired me. I ripped the envelope open and read from the sheet of paper:

Cafeteria Hamburger +
A Theory of Man and Woman —
SMS on Street = a fly on
the wall of . . .

"Huh!" I said sourly, after reading the clue over several times. "We've scared him." I passed the clue to Mal, who handed it to Jessi.

"How do you know?" asked Claudia.

"Because this clue makes no sense. I don't think it's even a real clue."

"'Cafeteria Hamburger' is a reference to lunch," said Stacey. She wrinkled her nose as if she could actually smell the canteen mystery meat.

"'A Theory of Man and Woman' is underlined *and* written as if it was the title of something," said Mal. "A film? No. Who'd make a film with a title like that?"

"Could be one of those badly translated French films?" said Abby.

"No," said Mal, giving Abby a Look. "More likely it's an article. Or a book. I say a book."

"But 'SMS on Street'? A fly on the wall? Give us a break!" said Abby. "I say we find Cary and we—"

"How about the street address of SMS?" suggested Jessi. "Elm Street?"

"Could be," I said.

Mary Anne had torn a sheet of paper from her notebook and was writing it all down. "Lunch reference, book title, street address, and still unsolved," she read aloud.

"I don't *like* flies," Stacey said to no one in particular.

"Maybe part of the clue is at each place," Mal mused. "You know, like the first part of the clue is in the canteen, the second part is in the library."

"But the third part would be the whole school," said Mary Anne. She frowned. "Unless it means right where the school meets the street, or something like that."

I looked at Claudia's clock (and thought dark thoughts about Cary and my watch). I looked at the phone, half daring it to ring. When it didn't I said, "Well, it's not much, but it's all we have to go on. We'll have a look tomorrow. Meanwhile. . ." I paused. The seconds ticked away. The clock flipped to 6:00. "This meeting of the BSC is hereby adjourned," I concluded.

"Hmmm," said Watson at breakfast.

Watson is not the biggest talker in the morning, so when he does speak, I know it must be important.

"Do you mean, hmmm, I need more milk? Or hmmm, where's the toast?" I asked.

He looked up from the newspaper he had spread out next to his cup of tea and smiled. "I meant, hmmm, that's some editorial in the mild-mannered *Stoneybrook News*."

The *Stoneybrook News* is a local paper, in case you hadn't guessed. It covers the local news, which always makes the front page, and the other, ordinary news, which gets less attention, unless it is something really important. (Watson and Mum subscribe to *The New York Times*, too, so they don't miss the rest of the picture.)

"What editorial?" I asked, instantly curious.

Watson pushed the paper towards me. I shoved my plate to the side and bent over the editorial page.

It was a sizzler, all about the lack of responsibility Stoneybrook's teachers and administrators were demonstrating, as evidenced by students' acts of vandalism and reckless behaviour in recent weeks. The piece made it sound as if SMS were under siege by evil students, while teachers cowered behind their desks.

"Wow!" I breathed.

"There are also letters," said Watson.

And indeed there were. One was from Mr Jerome Wetzler, a man who attended the Stoneybrook schools years ago and thinks everything these days is much too lax. He's written "Bring-back-the-old-days" letters before. Characteristically, he argued that the school budget should be cut even further. The teachers hardly did their work as it was. Why pay them for work they didn't do? That, apparently, would show the cowardly teachers and bad students what was what. In his day. . .

I skipped to the next letter.

Uh-oh! Mr Oates for Votes had written in, too. He talked a lot about himself—what a great and caring human being he was, and how he wanted what was best for everybody. Then he got down to business; the school board wouldn't even consider the teachers' demands, he wrote, "until order is restored to our once-proud school system".

Could a school system be proud? I wondered. I read on.

Miss Karush had also written in, pointing out that the teachers were not responsible for the acts of vandalism, and that the teachers' contracts and the vandalism were two separate issues that needed separate—and different—solutions.

Naturally, I agreed with Miss Karush. Teachers have it hard enough as is. I didn't understand how cutting money and staff would help the situation. It seemed as if it would just make it worse. But even more than that, I was afraid the worst was going to happen.

School in July.

In spite of the blistering editorial and the letters in the morning paper, school was uneventful. Before tutor time, we'd divided the different sections of Cary's clue among us, and agreed to check them out.

Just after midday, I asked my teacher if I could go to the toilet.

She nodded and pointed to a chart on the corner of her desk. "Sign out first," she said.

"Why?" I asked. "We've never done that before."

"New school policy. It's just to help us keep track of who is in and out of class if another, er, incident occurs."

"Oh. Right," I said. I signed out and made my way to the toilets.

As I left my classroom I thought I could hear footsteps running down the corridor, but I didn't see anyone. I didn't think any more about it until I turned the corner in the same direction the sound had come from—and found a puddle outside the toilet door.

"Ugh!" I said.

Then I realized that the puddle was growing.

Be brave! I told myself. It's not as bad as you think.

Gingerly avoiding any contact with the spreading puddle, I pushed the toilet door open. Inside, the floor was a lake. I could hear the sound of water running.

"Gross!" I said.

A hand clamped down on my shoulder. It was Miss Garcia, one of the teachers. "What's—" she began, then peered past me. "Quick—find one of the caretakers," she told me. "Hurry!"

I'd taken about two steps when I saw Mr Milhaus. "An emergency!" I practically shouted. "The girl's toilet is flooding!"

Mr Milhaus didn't even ask any questions. "I am here. Pardon me," he said, in his formal way, and stepped past Miss Garcia and me, into the spreading puddle. Less than a minute later, he came back out. "The basins have been plugged and the water left running," he said. "I have turned off the taps and shall mop."

"Thank you, Mr Milhaus," said Miss Garcia.

He nodded, and plunged back into the room.

I stared at his feet. Had they been wet *before* he went into the toilets the first time? And how did Mr Milhaus get to the scene so quickly?

Stop it, Kristy, I told myself. You suspect everybody of everything.

I stared absent-mindedly at the toilet door, trying to think where the nearest unflooded toilets were. Suddenly, I realized what I was staring at: another "MK", in green chalk, on the back of the toilet door.

"Green? Why green?" wondered Claudia out loud.

We were in the canteen. I had just told everybody about the flooded toilet incident and the newest green "MK" signature. "I mean, why did they switch to green? Did all their red marker pens run out?" Claud went on.

"If Dawn were here, she'd say green doesn't fit their aura," put in Mary Anne with a little smile. "Maybe someone is trying to frame the Mischief Knights."

"Or at least use them for cover," Stacey added.

Abby said, "Well, for your information, I was in another toilet just before lunch. By myself. *Until the door opened.*"

The dramatic way she said it got everybody's attention.

"Go on! Go on!" urged Claudia.

"Someone opened the door," Abby said, and stopped.

"GO ON!" we all said at the same time.

Abby shrugged. "Nothing much. A guy's voice said, 'Anybody in here?' I said, 'Yes', but before I could ask why a boy would want to know whether anybody was in the girls' toilets, I heard beeping noises, and the door closed again."

"He was going to flood your toilet, but you foiled him!" cried Claudia, in her best Nancy Drew manner.

"Maybe," said Abby. "I'm not sure, but it sounded as if whoever it was was trying to disguise his voice."

"You mean, it might not even have been a guy?" asked Stacey.

"No, it was a guy who didn't want to be recognized. The words were ... accented, or something."

"Mr Milhaus," I guessed, remembering my encounter with him.

"Maybe," said Abby again.

Stacey said, "Well, switching from Mischief Knights to Mystery Wars, I've checked out the library."

"I hope you had more luck than I did," said Mary Anne. She had hunted all over the canteen (getting some odd looks) before she fetched her lunch. Nothing.

Stacey beamed. "I looked up *A Theory of Man and Woman* in the card index. The library definitely has it, so I went to see if I could find the book on the shelf."

"The clue!" I interrupted.

"Wait." Stacey held up her hand. "No envelope. This, naturally, was a disappointment. So I stood there, holding the book, thinking about the equation— the whole clue. And that's when I saw the answer, right in front of me. It's a numerical clue."

"Uh-oh!" said Claudia.

"What are you talking about?" Mary Anne asked.

"You know—the number on a library book's spine—the classification. This book's number is three-zero-five. Each of the other clues has a number, too. We just have to work out which number fits each clue, then do the equation."

"A canteen hamburger has no number," said Abby. "*No* number. No value. In fact, at a dollar sixty-nine, it is a complete ripoff. It's disgusting . . ." She stopped, and a big grin broke out on her face. "It's number is one sixty-nine."

Mary Anne had whipped out her notebook and was writing everything down. "Does anybody know the school's street address?" she asked.

"Street address of the school: three hundred and fifty-eight Elm Street," said Abby. We looked at her in surprise.

"How did you know *that*?" I demanded.

"I filled in a million forms when I came to this school," said Abby. "I remembered."

Mary Anne read aloud: "One sixty-nine plus three-oh-five minus three fifty-eight equals. . ."

One sixteen," answered Stacey without hesitating.

"Room one sixteen!" I cried. "A fly on the wall of room one sixteen."

Abby leaped to her feet. "We have to check this *right now*."

In no time at all we'd got permission to leave the canteen, signed out (new policy there, too), and were on our way to room 116, which is a biology classroom. Sure enough, hanging on one of the walls was a big blown-up picture of a fly.

"Ugh!" said Stacey. "I don't like flies."

Claudia, giving it the artistic once-over, said, "It's quite amazing, you know."

I beat Abby by half a step to the picture, lifted it and found an envelope labelled "A true clue 4U" taped to the back of it.

Inside, the message was:

Nothing personal, Claudia, but check your spelling.

"Nothing personal!" said Claudia. "Huh! How personal can you get?"

"Have you got a spelling book? Some kind of workbook? A special dictionary?" Abby asked Claudia.

"I'll check my locker," said Claudia, still looking indignant. "But if Cary Retlin has broken into it to leave the next clue, he is going to be made into a *very* messy collage!"

Unfortunately, the warning bell rang before we could do any more brainstorming.

"Think about it in class," urged Abby. "You'll work it out."

That won a reluctant smile from Claudia. "Yes, and it'll beat thinking about classwork."

Claudia took Abby's advice. And Abby was right. I had just walked out of my last class when Claudia grabbed my arm and pulled me into the crowd. "Come on! We don't have much time. I hope they haven't closed."

"Who haven't, er, hasn't?" I asked. "Does this mean you've worked it out? The clue?"

"I *think* so. I think Cary must be talking about my old *Personals* column in the school newspaper. I used to use a computer to spellcheck the column. Spellcheck is amazing, except when you have two words that sound the same."

We were in luck. Emily Bernstein, the editor of the *SMS Express*, was sitting at a desk, going over copy with a pencil.

"Hey!" said Claudia.

"Hi, Claudia," said Emily, glancing up, then back down at the page of type with an intent, don't-interrupt-me look.

90

"Could I use that computer over there? Just for a moment?" asked Claudia.

"OK," replied Emily, without looking up again. "You know the drill. Just be sure to turn it off when you've finished. The *Express*'s computers are dinosaurs. They have new programs, though, for editing. . ." Her voice trailed off as she made another mark with her blue pencil.

Claudia switched on the computer, typed in her name—and jumped back when the computer said, "Welcome, Claudia!"

"Er, Emily? When did you teach the dinosaur to speak?"

Emily laughed. "That comes with the new software. It's a voice chip."

The screen flashed. Then two sentences appeared:

CLAUDIA, CHECK YOUR SPELLING! YOU HAVE THREE MINUTES!

"Eek!" said Claudia.

"Good grief!" I said.

"Spell 'potato'," said the computer.

Claudia typed in P-O-E-T-A-T-O-E.

"Wrong," said the computerized voice. "Spell 'potato'."

Claud, red-faced, glanced towards Emily. Emily was so intent on what she was doing that she hadn't heard a thing.

"Er, Claudia? Just leave out the e's," I said quickly.

Claudia typed in the correct spelling.

The computer made her spell six more words, all of them tricky, like "tomato" and "peculiar" and "embarrass".

"I think you should be able to spell peculiar any way you want to," said Claudia. "It goes with the definition."

I missed a couple, but between us we got them all.

Emily never even looked up.

Claudia grumbled through the whole thing. She kept talking back to the computer as if it were alive. It was pretty funny. But of course, I didn't laugh.

When the quiz was over, the screen flashed "WAIT A SECOND."

Then the next clue appeared.

B2 OR NOT B2 . . . THAT IS THE QUESTION.
{ARE YOU SITTING DOWN?}

Claudia pressed "print", and we had the clue in hard copy.

Just then, Emily finished what she'd been doing. She put aside the copy and walked over to us.

"Did I hear a spelling test just now?" she asked. (Which proves that Emily always pays attention. That's probably how she got to be editor of the *Express*.)

"Yep," said Claudia. "I bet you didn't

know the computer was programmed to do that, did you?"

"Cary Retlin," said Emily. "He's behind it."

We both must have looked surprised, because Emily explained, "He came in yesterday. Asked a lot of questions about you. . ."

She paused and grinned, giving Claudia a searching look. "Are you and Cary about to become *news*, Claudia?"

Claud shook her head, blushing slightly. "Forget it, Em," she said. "I don't like Cary Retlin. Not even a little bit. And he doesn't like me."

"Hmmm," said Emily, sounding just like Watson at breakfast. Then she said, "He said he'd heard you'd written a personals column for a while. He wanted to know about that. Then he offered to give me a few tips on some of our computer programs. He found so many glitches that I let him use one of our computers to work them out."

She looked over at the computer, then sat down and clicked away for a few moments. "Good," she said, after watching to see what happened. "He didn't mess up any of our programs." She pushed back her chair and said thoughtfully, "If he's clever enough to stick a spelling program in for you, Claudia, maybe he should be working for the *Express*."

We left Emily bent over the keyboard like a pianist, and headed out with our newest clue.

9th CHAPTER

So Jessi — the Thursday the kids led us on quite a dance during the scavenger hunt this afternoon, didn't they?

Ha, ha, Abigail. And yes. They were very creative ... not to mention original.

I mean, Buzzard Boys? Scavenger Queens ?? ??

The meeting place for the second leg of the great scavenger hunt was at Abby's house. Hannie and Linny Papadakis were there, as they live opposite. Tiffany and Maria Kilbourne, Shannon's younger sisters, came too. David Michael turned up, of course. Also the Hsu brothers, Timmy and Scott and Bill and Melody Korman, who live opposite me and one house up from the Papadakises.

They'd already divided up into teams by the time Abby and Jessi arrived. This was clear from the way they were lined up on either side of Abby's front steps. Anna was there too, talking to the kids as they waited for Abby and Jessi to arrive.

"Thanks," Abby said to her sister.

"No problem," replied Anna. She went indoors to practise her violin, and Jessi and Abby took over.

David Michael and Linny had wanted to be in the same team, as they are friends as well as neighbours. The other boys had also (surprise, surprise) taken a stand with them.

Sitting opposite the boys' team was the girls' team: Tiffany and Maria Kilbourne, Melody Korman and Hannie Papadakis.

"So it's boys versus girls, eh?" said Jessi.

Hannie answered, "There are more

people in the boys' team because they need more help."

"Huh!" scoffed David Michael.

"Double huh!" added Linny.

"We know all about the scavenger hunt," Hannie went on.

"We're ready to hunt for things the way buzzards do," said Tiffany.

Hannie pointed at the boys' team. "The Buzzard Boys," she said.

"Ha, ha, ha!" said Bill Korman, clearly not displeased with this team's new name.

"*We* are the Scavenger Queens," said Melody. She added proudly, "Maria and I thought of the name today at school."

It was clear that news of the scavenger hunt had got around. As Jessi and Abby explained the details most of the kids could hardly contain their excitement— or impatience.

"We know all that," Timmy Hsu burst out. "Can we see the list?"

"Is it school stuff?" interrupted Hannie.

"No." We'd decided against using the same themes, so that the kids couldn't plan ahead. Abby held up the two copies of that day's list. "Today our theme is sport." (Guess who chose that idea?)

"Cool!" said the boys. "We're gonna win."

Tiffany fixed the Buzzard Boys with a

steely eye. "You think you're the only ones who know about sport? Maria's an athlete, you know."

"Yeah," said Hannie.

"Yeah," said Jessi, trying to hide a smile.

Scott Hsu asked, "Can we start now? Please?"

Jessi read the first clue out loud: "You can bounce it, you can fling it, but with a racket you can't hack it."

"Easy, Scavenger Queens, you know what I mean?" Hannie said. She took off so fast that she nearly left Jessi behind.

The Buzzard Boys took off, too. In no time at all, both groups had acquired balls, the boys an old basketball from the Papadakises' house, the girls a football from Abby's. They'd quickly worked out that tennis balls and Ping-Pong balls wouldn't work.

The second clue was, "Even if you are a very good sport, this item stinks, on and off the court."

The boys were mystified. "*Nothing* about sport stinks," Scott Hsu said indignantly.

"A rotten referee or a crooked umpire," his brother suggested.

To which David Michael replied, "Where are we going to find a rotten referee or a crooked umpire?"

The girls were puzzled, too, Jessi told me later, but they tried to be practical. "A court is basketball, right?" asked Tiffany Kilbourne.

"Or tennis," said Hannie.

"My mum plays squash on a squash court," Melody piped up.

Silence.

"Maybe it's the player," Timmy Hsu was suggesting, over in the boys' camp. "A bad player stinks on and off the court."

"How are we supposed to find someone who admits he's a bad player?" demanded Linnie.

"And we couldn't collect him, anyway," added David Michael. "Not a human person."

The girls worked it out first. Tiffany said, "What about something you wear?"

Maria shrieked, "Underwear!" and the girls all began to laugh.

"I'm *not* collecting underwear," insisted Hannie.

"We can't go to someone's house and ask for. . ." Tiffany's voice trailed off. Her eyes lit up. "Socks. Old disgusting dirty. . ."

". . . icky, yucky, smelly, foot jelly," sang Hannie.

". . .socks!" the girls all shrieked.

They went to Mrs Porter's house and

asked for sports socks. Dirty ones. No such luck.

But the teenager who answered the door at the next house grinned and handed over her socks. "Keep 'em," she said.

"Thanks," Maria replied, taking the socks carefully. She turned to Jessi.

"You can carry the socks," said Jessi quickly. "I trust you."

The boys, too, had come up with underwear. Their next choice was gym shorts. Gym shorts were not as easy to come by as socks, and they had to make several stops before anyone could spare a pair. The shorts they eventually got hold of were old ones, but unfortunately (or fortunately, thought Abby, as she was carrying them) clean ones.

The next clue, "Go catch a fish, and make it swish," was of course a net.

Both teams met some resistance on this one. "A net? Certainly not," said one woman who answered the door and found Abby and the Buzzard Boys standing on her doormat. "No one wears hair nets any more."

"Hair nets?" said David Michael indignantly. "Who said anything about hair nets!"

At last someone gave the boys permission to cut down a piece of an old basketball net attached to a hoop at the back of the garage.

The girls tried to talk the owner of one huge house out of his tennis net, but he demurred. He ended up giving them the small fishing net that he used to scoop out his fish tank, laughing as he did so.

"It's clean," he said.

A look of alarm passed over Melody's face, but Maria said serenely, "Not like our socks!" and held them up for the man's approval.

Jessi managed to keep a straight face. Just.

The girls beat the boys back by one minute. This resulted in some friendly taunts.

"The Scavenger Queens rule," declared Hannie.

"It ain't over till it's over," said Linny folding his arms and trying to look like the famous baseball player Yogi Berra.

But hostilities ceased when Abby declared that there was just enough time for biscuits and juice at her house. Then their taunts turned to pleas—the Buzzard Boys and the Scavenger Queens wanted to meet again. And soon.

As experienced babysitters, Abby and Jessi knew better than to make promises they weren't sure they could keep. But they did agree that it had been fun.

101

And when the rest of us saw the boxes of items collected by the two teams, we all had to agree that this had been one of the BSC's more brilliant ideas.

10th CHAPTER

By Friday, Day Four of the Mystery War, I was feeling pretty pleased. So far, the BSC had been able to solve each of Cary's clues.

But although winning the Mystery War loomed large in my mind, it did *not* loom as large as the big, ugly black letters in the headline of the *Stoneybrook News* that morning at breakfast. Watson hadn't even said, "Hmmm." He'd just pushed it across the table for me to see.

TEACHERS TO STRIKE ON TUESDAY

"I can't believe it," Claudia moaned as we sat down to lunch that day. Naturally, this headline had not gone unnoticed by anyone's parents, or their kids.

Mary Anne said, "Dawn's supposed to come for a visit this summer. But if we have to go to school. . ."

"It's all the Mischief Knights' fault," I said grimly. "We have to stop them before they ruin summer for everybody."

"They are *so* stupid," said Claudia. "Don't they see that *they'll* have to go to summer school, too?"

Stacey said, "I'm still not convinced that they're behind the vandalism, you know. I mean, it's serious stuff, not pranks. Remember what we talked about the other day—the idea that somebody's trying to use them for cover? What about Brad Simon? Or Troy Parker? They've both been around a lot. I saw Brad coming out of the guidance office yesterday afternoon."

Mary Anne nodded. "Troy came by when Logan was shooting baskets a couple of days ago. He was saying some pretty nasty things about SMS, according to Logan."

"Anything about why SMS gave him a two-week suspension?" asked Abby, getting straight to the point as usual.

"No." Even kindhearted Mary Anne looked a little disappointed at not being able to tell Abby more about what kind of terrible trouble Troy might have been in.

"Well, maybe he thinks that since he's suspended, he can do whatever he wants," Abby observed. "I mean, they can't suspend him twice can they?"

"They can expel him," Claudia pointed out. "So forget *that*."

"Listen, let's not forget about *this* mystery." I held up the most recent clue. "B-two or not B-two . . . that is the question," I read aloud, to refresh everyone's memory.

"Didn't Shakespeare say that?" asked Claudia. Now it was her turn to grin. "Only he spelled it differently. Like two-bee or not two-bee?"

We all had to laugh at that.

Abby said, "So does this mean we look for places where Shakespeare can be found? Like, the library?"

"Or the classrooms, the ones in which teachers are teaching Shakespeare this term," suggested Mary Anne.

I reminded them of the second part of the clue: "Are you sitting down?"

That stumped us. Usually, when you ask someone if they are sitting down, you mean, be prepared for some really shocking news. But that didn't seem to fit here.

"Maybe you have to sit down to find the clue. Like when you work out which classroom or part of the library it might be in, you have to sit down to see it," suggested Abby.

Stacey wrinkled her nose. "That's pretty obscure," she said. "I mean, suppose you sat in the wrong chair? You'd miss it altogether."

"And wouldn't Cary like that," I muttered.

"That's it! That's it! Stace, you're a genius!" shouted Claudia.

"Thank you, but *what's* it?" asked Stacey, unfazed by Claudia going crazy right there at the lunch table.

"The right seat? Like when you buy tickets to plays and things, you have to sit in the right seat. Because the seats are all numbered."

"Seat B-two," I said. I gave Claudia a high-five.

"Most excellent, dude!" said Abby, in her best surfer's voice. "And of course the only numbered seats at SMS are in. . ."

"The assembly hall!" we all cried at once.

At that moment I felt it. A creeping sensation on my neck. I looked over my shoulder, and there was Cary Retlin, walking oh-so-casually past our table.

"Shhhh!" I commanded everyone.

But of course it was too late. Cary had heard us.

I wondered if he would sabotage us. I

didn't trust him one bit. Especially when he gave me that sly smile of his before he walked away.

"We have to get to the assembly hall. Right now!" I exclaimed. Visions of Cary beating us there danced in my head.

"Too late now," said Abby. "Lunch is over."

Sad but true. We would have to wait. I comforted myself with the knowledge that Cary had to go to class now, as well.

But I knew that Cary was sneaky in the extreme. If he wanted to sabotage this clue, he'd find a way.

The moment the last bell of the day rang, we flew from our classrooms like homing pigeons, not even stopping at our lockers. We were breathing hard, as if we'd been in a race, when we reached the assembly hall door.

Abby yanked it open and we stampeded down the aisle.

There, taped under seat B2, was the usual white envelope with the patonizing words, "Clue—in case you hadn't noticed" printed on the front.

As I was reaching for it, I heard Mal, who was behind me, say, "You know, Abby. Like the beeps on a watch."

I turned, momentarily distracted. "What?"

"Abby and I were talking about the toilet incidents yesterday and I was just telling Abby that as she was in the toilet at midday, maybe the beeping sounds she heard were the beeps from a watch, set to beep every hour."

"Like *my* watch," I said. "That proves it. That proves it's Cary Retlin."

"Calm down, Kristy," said Claudia. "It just proves that whoever it was has a watch that beeps. And everybody's watch does that these days."

It was true. Although I was convinced in my heart that this was another nail in the coffin of proof I was constructing in which to bury Cary, I had to agree that it wasn't conclusive evidence.

I turned back and reached for the envelope again.

This time a loud voice shouted, "What the—"

I jerked my hand back.

Someone screamed. Something crashed.

We all jumped.

"Behind the curtain!" gasped Mary Anne, pointing.

Words like "sabotage" and "Cary" and "uh-oh!" went through my head. But before I could act, the door next to the stage opened, and Mr Kingbridge walked in with a group of adults, among them Mr

108

Oates and a woman who was holding a micro-cassette recorder.

"I'm glad that the *News* is taking an interest in this problem, Miss Bernstein," Mr Oates said in a clear, carrying voice.

Miss Bernstein just nodded.

Another crash, another scream.

Mr Kingbridge jumped on to the stage without hesitation and yanked the curtain aside.

We gasped at the chaos that met our eyes.

The scenery from the last school play, which had been propped against the back wall, had been torn apart, some of it shredded. And the props—furniture, rugs, a bicycle and a ladder—had been tied together in the centre of the stage with the ropes used to move the backstage props around. The knots looked numerous, and huge. Someone would probably need a saw to cut through the heavy rope.

We hurried forward. We stopped.

Clearly visible in the middle of the stage floorboards, in front of the tied-up furniture, were the letters "MK" in green chalk, although a different shade from the green I'd seen on the toilet door.

"What's the meaning of this?" demanded Mr Kingbridge in an angry voice.

"Out of control! See?" exclaimed Mr

Oates to the *Stoneybrook News* reporter. She was raising a camera to take pictures.

Just then Mr Milhaus came hurrying down the aisle on the far side of the assembly hall, carrying his mop and bucket. "I shall clean it up," he said. "Do not worry. It shall be dealt with."

He's destroying evidence, I thought. But before I could put the thought into words, Mr Oates turned, pointed at us, and said, "AHA!"

The other adults turned in our direction.

"Aha?" repeated Claudia. "What does that mean?"

"It means guilty, guilty, guilty," muttered Abby.

Mr Kingbridge frowned, slipping into his school disciplinarian mode. "Kristy. Claudia . . . what are all you girls doing in the assembly hall?" he asked.

"I should think *that* would be obvious," said Mr Oates. He turned to the reporter. "Go on, take their picture! SMS vandals."

"No way!" I cried. And then I realized that of course, Cary Retlin had sabotaged us after all. Set us up. Framed us to take the blame. He knew we'd be coming to the hall after school. So he made his mischief, told someone about it and waited for us to be caught.

110

Steaming, I said in a loud voice, "We didn't have anything to do with this. Use that camera to photograph the evidence, not us."

Mr Kingbridge said, "Let's not jump to any conclusions."

I said, "Mr Kingbridge, may I—no, may *we* speak to you privately for a moment?"

A few minutes later, we were standing with Mr Kingbridge on one side of the hall, and I was telling him all about Cary: how he'd taken my watch, how he'd erased my maths homework and how he'd been absent from Stacey's class when the second fire alarm was set off. I told him about Abby hearing a beeping watch in the cloakroom, too.

Mr Kingbridge had pulled a small notepad out of his coat pocket. He jotted down notes as I talked, and when I had finished, he took down all our names.

"Very well," he said. "I don't think you girls are involved. You can go. And I'll give Cary Retlin a call."

We made a hasty exit (after a quick, unobtrusive detour to pick up the clue from under seat B2).

"That'll teach him," I said when we were outside.

Claudia shook her head. "I don't know, Kristy. If Cary's not the troublemaker, you might have got him into a lot of trouble he didn't deserve.

"He's guilty," I insisted. I was still furious over being set up. "Believe me, Cary Retlin is guilty."

11th CHAPTER

When the doorbell rang that afternoon at Claudia's house, just after I'd called the last BSC meeting of the week to order, none of us paid any attention. Mary Anne, Stacey, Mal and I were digging through the items the four teams of kids had found in the scavenger hunt while Jessi wrote in the club notebook and Abby made horrible jokes. And Claudia, of course, was passing around junk food, in this case mint chocolate M&M's and All Natural Potato Crisps.

"This is a disgusting combination," remarked Mal, munching on a mixture of the two.

"The crisps are good," said Stacey.

Someone knocked at Claudia's door. "Low profile," she warned, and we put the junk food out of sight as she opened the door.

Janine stood there. "Someone is here to see Kristy," she said.

"Me?"

"Yes."

"Who?"

"He didn't say," replied Janine. She turned and left as I stood up.

"He?" I wondered.

"Go and see who it is," said Mary Anne practically. "That's the best way to find out."

"Bother!" I said and went down the stairs to find. . .

Cary Retlin, standing just inside the front door. He didn't look very pleased to see me. In fact, he looked even less pleased to see me than I was to see him.

"Thanks a lot, Kristy," he said.

"What?"

"I have a few things to say to you, and then I'll go." He held up his hand and ticked off his fingers as he talked.

"One, I was in class when the toilets were flooded, as my teacher will tell you. I don't have any telepathic powers, so telekinetically turning on taps and blocking the basins is out of the question. Two, I was in class when the first fire alarm was set off, which also can be confirmed by my teacher, and I was in the guidance office when the second alarm was set off, which is why Stacey didn't see me in class.

Three, today this afternoon, when the stage in the assembly hall was vandalized, I was tutoring a sixth-grader in maths. If you want a sworn affidavit from him, I could probably arrange it. Four, not only would I never destroy a car, but if I ever wanted to, I wouldn't make the stupid mistake of not finding out who the car belonged to before I did it. I know which car Mr Kingbridge drives, not that I have anything against Mr Kingbridge."

He lowered his hand to put his fists on his hips. "If you have any doubts about whether I'm telling you the truth, you can give Mr Kingbridge a call. I've just left him at his office, where he and I spent two hours of 'quality time' together, thanks to you. I thought you were a better 'investigator', Kristy. If you had a licence, I'd probably ask that it be revoked."

I was shocked. Stunned. And mortified. Now that Cary was finally denying his involvement in the vandalism, I knew he was telling the truth. And I felt awful for being a tell-tale, like some little kid. I tried to say something, but Cary cut me off.

"Let me finish. Just for your information, Mr Kingbridge rang all of my teachers about what you'd told him, and my parents. My parents were not happy, even though Mr Kingbridge did come to the conclusion that I wasn't responsible for any of the things you so confidently accused me of. He *did* say I had to return your watch. So here."

Cary thrust the watch at me. I looked down at it, then up at Cary.

"Er, Cary, I'm sorry. The other BSC members didn't think I should tell Mr Kingbridge about everything. But I thought you'd set us up to get caught in the assembly hall."

"I wouldn't do that," said Cary. He smiled a very faint smile. "Lacks subtlety."

"Whatever. I am sorry. I have a big mouth sometimes and I speak without thinking."

Cary shrugged.

"Keep the watch," I said. "Until we solve your mystery."

The old smile came back. "You mean *if* you solve my mystery," he said and left, as usual, before I could answer.

I went back upstairs, where I was bombarded with questions from everyone, especially after they heard who my visitor had been.

"Wow!" said Abby. "Way to go, Kristy!"

I felt my face redden. But I couldn't really be annoyed with Abby. She was right.

"You apologized," said Mary Anne. "You did the right thing."

"True. And I told Cary to keep my watch—until we win the Mystery War." I grinned. "You know what he said? '*If* you win.'"

"So I suppose his two hours of 'quality time' with Mr Kingbridge didn't slow him down much," said Stacey.

"It would slow *me* down," said Mal.

"Yes. I'd rather dance in front of a hostile audience than spend *two hours* being interrogated in the school office," Jessi added.

"Well, we're back to where we started," I said. "Cary's not the one behind the vandalism. Somebody seems to be using the Mischief Knights as cover. We don't have any idea who it is. And there are only two school days left till the teachers go on strike."

"Let's go over the clues and our ideas again," Claudia suggested.

We all groaned, and Mary Anne grabbed a piece of paper. But Mal said, "Stop. I realized last night that I should have been writing about both mysteries in the mystery notebook all along. So I worked on it for an hour or so and brought it up to date." She held up the mystery notebook we'd started when we'd been stalked by a particularly nasty character.

"And a review of it could help us take a fresh look at the vandalism mystery."

"Great," said Mary Anne.

Mal flipped the notebook open to the heading "Vandals", and took notes as we talked.

"OK, it's not Cary," I said. "And it's not the real Mischief Knights."

"And if it's not Cary, is it any student at SMS?" asked Jessi. "I mean, if the cloakroom was flooded during class time, it wouldn't be a student who signed himself or herself out, because that would point to who did it."

Abby suggested, "Old Oates for Votes could have done it. You know, the way he turned up with that reporter as the MKs struck was awfully convenient, don't you think?"

I could tell Abby liked the idea of Mr Oates's being the culprit, maybe even as much as I had liked the idea of blaming everything on Cary.

I suddenly pictured Mr Milhaus, hurrying into the assembly hall that afternoon. And just as suddenly, I saw the mop and bucket that I had almost fallen over after the fire drill—and the wet floor. Just that one spot, near the fire alarm.

I hadn't seriously considered Mr Milhaus as the culprit, but what if he were? I told everybody about the mop and bucket and the wet floor. Mal said, "Mr Milhaus? Why?" then answered her own question. "He *was* upset on the night of the meeting, about the budget cuts that would affect the caretakers. Maybe he's doing all this to keep his job. You know, to make himself seem indispensable."

It seemed possible. Outrageous, true, but possible.

Claudia wasn't buying it, though. "That's rather extreme, don't you think? I vote for Brad Simon and Troy Parker. They're not even supposed to be at SMS, but they always are, especially when something weird happens."

"And don't forget all the nasty things Troy was saying about SMS and Mr Kingbridge, that day Logan shot baskets with him," added Mary Anne. She hesitated. "But it's still not a deciding factor. There are good arguments in favour of each suspect."

Mal turned a page. Everyone else was quiet. Then she looked up. "We should check the beeping watch clue," she said. "Tomorrow. See who has a watch, and whether it's the kind that beeps."

It was better than nothing. We agreed to that, answered some phone calls and finished off the M&M's and most of the crisps. Eventually we had a chance to look at the clue Cary had left taped under seat B2.

It read:

Hey Abby.
I PA2+FotUSoAand2+R

(look up)

"OK, that's it. This clue makes NO SENSE," said Abby.

"We'll work it out," I said, with more confidence than I felt. I stared at the drawing of the four witches. We all copied the clue down, so we could think about it over the weekend.

Then Claudia's clock rolled over to 6:00, and I adjourned the meeting.

And left thinking that maybe Cary wasn't the green Mischief Knight, but he definitely knew how to cause trouble.

12th CHAPTER

Sunday

awsome. Scavinger hunts are realy art reserch. I totaly luved it. Didnt you, Mary Ann?

Claudia, I have to agree about the awesome part. But I'm not so sure that everything we found qualifies as Art.

For the theme of the final part of the scavenger hunt, Claudia and Mary Anne had chosen nature.

Saturday was sunny and breezy, a nice morning for a nature-themed scavenger hunt. Parents on their way to do errands, or to play sports themselves, dropped the kids off at Claudia's house. Mrs Prezzioso, dressed in a snow-white tennis outfit, left Jenny, who was dressed in perfectly ironed dungarees with a red bandanna tied around her neck, a crisp, white, scalloped-edge T-shirt, red socks trimmed with white lace and spotless white tennis shoes. Claudia, with her keen fashion sense, could tell that this was Mrs Prezzioso's (and Jenny's) idea of what to wear to a scavenger hunt. The younger Hobarts, James aged eight, Mathew, aged six, and Johnny aged four, arrived wearing more casual attire—jeans, heavily patched or in need of patches, and an assortment of faded T-shirts. They waved as their father drove away with their oldest brother, Ben.

"He's going to football practice," explained James. Then he grinned. "What you Yanks call soccer." (The Hobarts are from Australia.)

Becca, Jessi's eight-year-old sister, turned up on her bike, together with her best friend Charlotte Johanssen, who is also eight. The last two to arrive were seven-year-old Rosie Wilder, a one-time child actor but at the moment looking mostly like a kid who was ready to have a good time, and lastly four-year-old Jamie Newton, who ran across the lawn calling, "Claudee Kishi, Claudee Kishi!" and flung his arms around her. Jamie, easy-going and very affectionate, is one of the BSC's favourite kids.

Claudia and Mary Anne had to give the kids only the most basic explanation of the scavenger hunt. Not only had word got around, but the Hobarts had already decided on a name for their team: The Klue Krushers.

"Get it?" said James. "Like Kristy's Krushers!"

Everyone loved the name and immediately wanted to be on the Klue Krushers team. But eventually Claudia and Mary Anne persuaded the kids that they needed two teams to play, and that the other team could think up their own name. With much tact, they persuaded James and Becca to be on the team with Johnny and Jenny, and Charlotte and Rosie to be on the team with Jamie and Mathew. The team with the most Hobarts won the right to be the Klue Krushers. That left Charlotte and Rosie to think up their own team name, with the help of their teammates.

"How about the Killers?" said Charlotte bloodthirstily, giving the Klue Krushers a look.

"I bet you can think of something funnier," said Mary Anne.

"I like Scavenger Queens," Becca offered.

"It's been taken, Becca," said Charlotte impatiently.

"I don't want to be a Queen," insisted Jamie.

"What about the Buzzard Bashers?" said Rosie.

Everyone liked that, particularly as the Bashers are also the main rivals of the Krushers softball team.

The names having been settled, Mary Anne outlined the rules and then Claud, as head of the Klue Krushers, read the first clue out loud from her list: "This sings in the trees and floats in the breeze; a part or a whole will fulfil this role."

The two teams set off in opposite directions.

Naturally the Klue Krushers thought it would be a great idea to catch a bird. Claud dissuaded them from that idea, pointing out that it would take too much time.

"Does anyone in the neighbourhood have a canary or a parrot?" asked James. "Maybe we could borrow one."

In the other group, Mary Anne was listening to a similar conversation. Only the Buzzard Bashers wanted to pool their money and go to a pet shop, to see if they could buy a bird.

As Claud had with the Krushers, Mary Anne talked the Buzzard Bashers out of the notion, wondering as she did so if maybe the clue had been too difficult.

Then Charlotte exclaimed triumphantly, "Feathers!"

At about the same time, Becca was saying, "Wind chimes!" and pointing to a wind chime mobile that Claud had made out of all kinds of found objects, including spoons, bits of wood, shells and, yes, feathers. It was hanging on the Kishis' front porch. Claud had given it to her mother for Mother's Day. She decided her mum wouldn't mind lending it to a good cause, and borrowed it.

Janine, who was reading on the front porch, warned the Klue Krushers to return it safely.

"We will," promised Jenny.

"No problem, mate," piped up Johnny.

Janine raised an eyebrow. "Australia. The Sydney opera house is quite extraordinary," she commented, and went back to her book.

Claudia was impressed with her team's

creativity. The wind chimes definitely sang in trees and floated in the breeze.

Meanwhile, Mary Anne was resigning herself to carrying an old feather pillow that one of the neighbours had laughingly donated.

The next clue was: "It's icky, it's gooey, it's stinky, it's a stew. If you look down at the ground then you will figure out this clue."

Charlotte immediately wrinkled her nose. "I have to clean up after Carrot in our garden. Is that the clue?" (Carrot is the Johannsens' pet schnauzer.)

Becca, together with Claudia, was echoing almost the same sentiments. "Oh, yuck! Is that clue dog poo?"

Mary Anne and Claudia each quickly disposed of that idea before it could go anywhere. (Actually, we had been thinking about mud.)

Both groups (with a little help from Claudia and Mary Anne) eventually settled on jars of mud (phew!).

"Whenever I'm seen, I'm always green; from winter through fall, I don't shed at all," Claudia read aloud, keeping an eye on her watch. "We just have time for one more."

"The garden gnome!" shouted Mathew.

"What?" asked Claud, considerably

startled. She looked in the direction he was pointing. Sure enough, almost hidden among the bushes at one side of Kristy's old house was an ornamental statue. It was an elf in a green suit.

"We *can't* borrow the garden gnome," said Claudia. Not only did she not know who it belonged to, but she didn't want to carry it. It looked heavy. "Besides, what does he have to do with nature?"

"He's in a garden," argued Becca.

But Claudia stood firm. The Klue Krushers finished up with the more conventional solution, a branch from a fir tree.

The Buzzard Bashers? Well, they thought of a branch from an evergreen, too, but they rejected it. Not in favour of a lawn gnome, but in favour of . . . a square of Astro Turf donated by a neighbour.

Mary Anne only just kept herself from laughing. It was, after all, green all the year round. And as artificial grass, it probably did, somehow, come under the heading "nature".

After the strenuous exertions of the morning, it was time for some refreshment. Claudia, of course, had arranged to have a good supply of "healthy" junk food on hand. Meanwhile, some of the kids from the other teams had begun to arrive, together with the other members of the BSC.

I hopped out of Nannie's Pink Clinker, accompanied by Abby and Shannon, who helped me carry the boxes of clues from the first four teams. Behind me came David Michael, and Hannie and Linny Papadakis. Mal and Jessi arrived with a Pike contingent, and Logan rode up moments later on his bike.

So while the teams ate oatmeal biscuits and lemonade, and boasted about how well they'd done (Logan and Mary Anne volunteered to keep an eye on them all), the rest of the BSC members and I went into Claudia's room to ponder the clues.

Claudia opened the discussion with the observation that we were going to have a tough time deciding among the teams and declaring any solutions "better" than others. She secretly gave the wind chimes high marks, though, and was attracted to the AstroTurf concept. "It's like bad art imitating life," she said.

Abby immediately shot back, "Whose life?"

Actually, we all agreed that the best solutions were the AstroTurf, the wind chimes, the dirty socks, the slightly wilting tree branch (not the evergreen—the one that stood for paper) and the trainers. But how many points should we give each thing? Naturally, each babysitter was in favour of giving the most points to her team.

After a while, I put my hands over my ears. If I hadn't been so caught up in the mystery and the Mystery War, I would have organized an objective point-based system ahead of time. But it wasn't too late. "Enough arguing!" I said. I took a piece of paper and began writing down numbers—points for finishing, points for the most clues, points for the best items. Then I handed it over to Stacey. "Add it up, please."

Stacey added it up in about two seconds. She smiled. "It's close, but the winner is . . . the Scavenger Queens!"

Jessi pirouetted and then waved her arms in the air.

Claudia said, "Well, I think we should give the AstroTurf honourable mention. And the wind chimes."

"Good idea," I agreed. "We'll give honourable mentions for the best items, OK?"

Everybody liked that idea. We went back downstairs to announce the results.

It's amazing how fast a whole kitchen full of kids can quieten down when you are going to announce the winner of a competition.

I gave them the speech about all of them doing a good job.

They squirmed.

I spoke of creativity and inspiration. They grew restless.

At last I announced the winners.

They went ballistic. "Yeah!" shouted Hannie. "Queens rule!"

"Buzzards rule!" retorted Adam.

"Buzzard Bashers! Buzzard Bashers!" chanted Charlotte in her best cheerleader style.

"*Quiet!*" commanded Mal.

It worked.

Then someone said, "We demand a rematch!" and it started all over again.

The scavenger hunt had been a success. A rousing, noisy success.

13th CHAPTER

On Monday morning I woke up with a feeling of dread. Practically my first thought was, "The strike. Oh, no!"

Only one more day before the teachers walked out, if they didn't have a contract.

Luckily, Watson wasn't at breakfast. He'd left early on business. That meant that the newspaper had left with him. So I didn't feel obliged to see if another story about the battle between the board of education and the teachers was on the front page, or read the letters from various indignant citizens on both sides of the issue.

On the bus to school, the kids in the back seemed a little rowdier than usual, even for a Monday morning. I registered the noise level in one corner of my mind as Abby and I pondered the most recent and most obscure clue from Cary.

131

"USoA *has* to be United States of America. I mean, what else could it be?" demanded Abby.

I had to agree. I had come to the same conclusion. We stared hard at the piece of paper, as if our eyes could burn out some hidden letters in invisible ink. Of course, that didn't work. But after a while Abby said, "If the lower-case 'o' stands for 'of', then maybe the lower-case letters all stand for short words. For example, the 't' could stand for 'the'."

"It's worth a try," I said.

It isn't easy writing on the Wheeze Wagon, but in between the lurches, and whenever it came to a stop, I wrote on the back of my notebook, "IPA2 the F of the United States of America and 2 the R (WITCHES) (look up)."

"Well, the 2 could stand for 'to' then," I said. I crossed out the "2s" and wrote "to".

Abby and I both said, instantly, "The Pledge of Allegiance."

"I pledge allegiance to the flag of the United States of America," said Abby. Then she stopped.

We looked at the crude drawing of the witches. Abby said, "Frankly, these witches are typical witch stereotypes. Pointed hats. Crooked noses. Bad hair. Fashion-victim clothes. These four witches stand for something . . . the original meaning of the word witch . . . four witches!" *Four witches stand.*

I started to laugh. Of course. The four witches meant "for which it stands."

The bus lurched to a halt in front of the school. The steps were strangely empty.

"You lot are going to have to hurry," the bus driver told us. "We're a little behind schedule today."

"The Pledge of Allegiance," I said. "The clue is. . ."

"In the flag, I bet. It says 'look up' and that's what you look up to when you say the pledge," finished Abby. "And Cary is in my tutor group and . . . we're going to be late!"

We flew off the bus and went up the front steps of the school at a run. "Go!" I cried, and Abby sped down the corridor to her tutor room as I turned the corner and ducked into mine.

I learned later that Abby had looked up and seen the note. The moment tutor time was over, while the teacher wasn't looking, she jumped up and grabbed the small white square tucked into the metal sleeve holding the flag. She whipped around, holding it triumphantly aloft, but Cary had vanished from the room, so she couldn't flaunt her victory.

She unfolded the note and read, "Bring

me the head of the False Mischief Knights!"

With that clue, the two mysteries had dovetailed into one. The final clue in the Mystery War, and the way to keep school from going into the middle of summer were coming down to one and the same thing: the BSC had to find the SMS vandal.

Through the BSC grapevine, we quickly spread the word of the final clue, and the final challenge. I paused briefly to wonder if Cary himself knew who the vandal was, and if he was going to turn the culprit in if we didn't. Or did he think going to school in the middle of the summer was another one of those complications that makes life interesting?

We spent the rest of the morning doing a "watch check": trying to find out who had a digital watch that beeped. Stacey asked Mr Milhaus what time it was (after not-so-subtly tracking him down in the corridor between classes). He pulled out an old-fashioned pocket watch to consult it.

Mary Anne spotted Brad Simon in the guidance office and saw immediately that he was wearing a *large* digital watch. Not only that, but he was standing with the woman Abby had noticed during one of the false fire alarms. Before her head knew what her feet were doing, Mary Anne was walking into the office to pick up a couple of those guidance counsellor brochures that no one ever reads. As she did so, one of the inside doors opened, and the guidance counsellor said, "Brad? Mrs Simon?" Mrs Simon put her hand on Brad's shoulder and marched him ahead of her into the office.

Could Brad have eluded his *mother* to set off the fire alarm? It seemed unlikely.

Once again we met at lunch to discuss the clues.

We were feeling pretty frustrated.

"It's like a sort of clue soup," I said, "and worse. I mean, none of it goes together. It's like putting sugar and salt in the same recipe."

Claudia sat down next to me and remarked, "Sugar and salt are good together. Like potato crisps and chocolate."

We all groaned.

Claudia laughed and said, "Guess what, you lot. False Mischief Knights news. Emily Bernstein has just received a letter from a Mischief Knight. In dark green. For publication. The writer says that everyone at the school is unfair and he—or she—hopes the strike does take place."

"Oh, grow *up*!" said Abby impatiently,

meaning the writer of the letter, not Claud. "The world is unfair. And people like this creep just make it worse, always blaming other people for their own problems."

"No kidding," Stacey said. "Because 'unfair' is unhappy, we all have to be unhappy, too."

"Well, whoever this green MK is, they're not staying on top of things. Attention to detail is crucial in crime," I said.

"Translate, please," said Mary Anne with a little smile.

"He's not paying attention to details. He uses green to sign his messages, not red, like the real MKs. He damages the wrong car, the light green one instead of the red one. I mean, come on."

Mary Anne's eyes widened. "Colours," she said.

Claudia looked up. "Yes?"

"Colours. Red and green . . . the False MK is *colour blind!*"

"Well, that would explain it," said Stacey, laughing. "An ingenious theory, Sherlock Spier."

"I'm serious," said Mary Anne, her cheeks flushing now. "I mean it."

I said slowly, "It's a possibility."

"Hey!" Claudia shouted. "Hey! She's right! You're right, Mary Anne!"

We all jumped about a mile.

"Claudia!" Stacey complained.

"It's Troy Parker. Think about the way he dresses! Fashion-victim basics. He never *ever* matches. And the mismatches aren't deliberate. If he was colour blind, that would explain it."

"Statistically speaking, males are much more likely to be colour blind than females," remarked Stacey, sounding a little like Janine.

Jumping up, Abby announced, "The mystery is solved. The school is saved. Mr Kingbridge, here we come!"

I grabbed her arm. "Wait."

"What?" said Abby.

"We've—I've—already accused the wrong person once. I don't want to do that again. We need more proof," I said.

"But how?" asked Mary Anne.

"Check Troy's locker for proof," said Stacey. "Green chalk. Green paint."

"Yes, right. And who here can break into a locker?" said Abby sarcastically.

In the pause that followed, all of us must have been thinking the same thing.

Cary Retlin.

"OK, OK," I said, standing up. "I'll find him and ask him. But I won't like it."

"Think of the school," urged Claudia. "Think of *summer school*."

* * *

I tracked Cary down after school.

I wondered if he slept with that mocking smile pinned to his lips.

I said, "We've solved the mystery. But we need proof. We need you to open a locker for us so we can get it."

"What makes you think I know how to break into lockers?" Cary asked, slamming his own locker shut and locking it, as if for emphasis.

"You have before," I reminded him, referring to a past mystery in which Cary had demonstrated lock-loosening skills.

He didn't acknowledge that. Instead he said, "Even if I could open a lock, why should I trust you? You could be setting me up for Mr Kingbridge."

I went red. He didn't trust me. It seemed weird to realize that as much as I didn't trust Cary, he felt the same way about me. "You're right. I could be. But I acted without thinking before. This is different."

"If I help you, then you haven't solved the mystery entirely without my help," he pointed out. "The BSC will forfeit the Mystery War."

Again, he was right. I hesitated for a long moment. But how could I not agree? We had no other way to stop Mr Oates's campaign against SMS, and therefore, the strike.

I nodded slowly. "OK," I said. "We'll forfeit. It's worth it."

Mary Anne zoomed over to us. "We've found his locker," she said.

I looked at Cary. He didn't ask whose locker. He just nodded. "You forfeit, I'm in," he said.

"I saw Troy Parker a few minutes ago." Mary Anne panted as we hurried down the corridor as fast as we could without arousing teacher-type suspicion. "He was wearing a watch just like the one you have."

"Had," I couldn't help saying.

Cary laughed.

Claudia stood guard at one end of the corridor with Stacey. Mal and Jessi took the top and bottom of the stairs and Abby and Mary Anne took the other end of the corridor. I followed Cary and watched as he knelt by the locker and went to work.

14th
CHAPTER

I don't know how he did it, though I swear
I watched him like a hawk, but moments
later, Cary had the locker open.

"Amazing, eh?" said Cary.

Ignoring him, I peered into the locker.

The first thing I saw was a big green
permanent marker pen. I reached in, took
it out by one end (hoping I wasn't ruining
any fingerprints) and held it aloft. Abby
nodded, and she and Mary Anne took off.
I knew they were going to fetch Mr Kingbridge.

"Oh, ho!" said Cary. "Troy's guilty—
and he's a Boy Scout!"

A row of Boy Scout badges on a neck-
tie had been wadded up on the floor of
the locker. Knot-tying, I thought, remembering the stage sabotage. Something
every Boy Scout has to learn.

140

Then I saw it. An envelope addressed to the *Stoneybrook News*. I picked it up, but before I could open it I heard an agitated squeak from Claudia and Stacey's end of the corridor. I looked in their direction and saw that they were pointing and waving frantically.

From behind me a voice said, "What are you doing?"

I leaped to my feet, still clutching the envelope. I turned to face Troy Parker.

He looked very angry.

I swallowed. Cary somehow seemed to melt back and blend in with the lockers. I was facing Troy on my own.

"This envelope," I said. "Inside I bet there's a copy of the letter *you* sent to the SMS *Express*."

Troy took a step forward, his fists clenched.

Uh-oh! I thought.

Then his shoulders drooped and his eyes looked suddenly scared, like a little kid's.

Claudia's voice said, "You're colour blind aren't you, Troy?"

Troy's head jerked up. "How did you know?"

"You mixed up the colours of the car you vandalized. I think you realized that. And the Mischief Knights sign everything in red, not green."

"You're finished, man," Cary chimed in.

"So?" shouted Troy. "So what? And so what if I am suspended? Kingbridge is a liar. A complete liar. I didn't steal anything. And I don't have an attitude. Denying that you're a thief doesn't mean you have an attitude!"

Attitude? He had a chip on his shoulder the size of a log, I thought.

Troy ranted on, "I hope the teachers do strike! And they have to work all summer. No, I hope they all get fired. And the administration. It would serve everybody right. Let someone else take the blame for a change!"

I let Troy talk. I couldn't think of anything to say.

Besides, Mr Kingbridge had come quietly down the corridor with Abby and Mary Anne. He was listening to every word.

He put a hand on Troy's shoulder.

Troy turned his head, saw who was there, and closed his mouth with a snap. A sullen look came over his face.

"Thank you, Kristy," said Mr Kingbridge with remarkable calm. "Thank you all. Troy, I think it would be best if you came with me now."

Troy went quietly.

But just before Mr Kingbridge left, he

looked at Cary standing next to me, and glanced at his wrist. He raised an eyebrow. "That is *your* watch, isn't it, Cary?" he asked.

"Yes," I answered quickly.

I waited until Mr Kingbridge and Troy were out of earshot to add, "I suppose the war is over. It was fun while it lasted."

"And I suppose it's time to give your watch back, even if you don't really deserve it," said Cary. He slid it off his wrist and handed it to me.

"Thanks," I replied, and I really meant it. I fastened the watch on my own wrist and immediately felt more organized. It was a beautiful feeling.

"But don't think this lets the BSC off the hook. You lot need me. I keep you from becoming complacent. Boring."

"*Boring?*" I said, outraged.

But before I could say anything else, Cary, as usual, had walked away.

I put my hands on my hips and glared after him. The Mystery War had been only a battle, after all.

The war between the BSC and Cary Retlin was still on.

"This emergency meeting of the Stoneybrook School Board has been called to announce that the SMS vandal—one disgruntled student who is not at *all* representative of our student body—has been apprehended. Appropriate measures are being taken, and I think it is time we stopped letting our negotiations be side-tracked by what has become, essentially, a non-issue," said Miss Karush.

As applause broke out, Mr Oates leaped to his feet.

The BSC, out in force and in the front row, applauded still louder, trying to drown out Mr Oates.

But eventually he prevailed. Glaring at the audience, he said, "I protest. How do we know that this is an isolated incident? How can we be sure that the teachers haven't conveniently chosen a scapegoat on which to hang these acts, in order to protest themselves? How—"

"Don't be ridiculous, Oates," interrupted a short woman who had been Mr Oates's ally at the previous meeting. "Are you accusing the teachers of framing someone?"

Mr Oates's mouth opened and closed, like the mouth of a big, fat fish out of water. "B-but, but. . ." he spluttered.

"Sit down!" said the woman.

The audience rocked the rafters with cheers and applause.

Mr Oates sat down.

Miss Karush took over again. Debate followed. Lots of talk, much of it not worth repeating. (Except for Mr Milhaus's passionate plea not to cut the maintenance budget of the buildings. It turns out he'd personally overseen SMS for over thirty years.)

But the upshot of the discussion was that the teachers agreed not to go on strike, and the school board made noises about being sure they'd be able to reach a compromise before the school year was over, without any maintenance cuts.

Mr Kingbridge stopped us on the way out. "Thank you again," he said. "And good work."

"Just another day at school for us," I said.

"As long as it's not summer school," added Claudia, and we all began to laugh.

So on Tuesday morning, school was back to normal. The bus groaned and wheezed, Abby complained about the pollen count, and we argued about baseball. I saw Logan and Mary Anne walking up the steps to school arm in arm, and paused a moment to admire Claudia's outfit as she stood talking to Mal and Jessi. I waved at Stacey and Robert (Stacey's boyfriend) and bounded into the door of the school.

Summer was coming. I was happy.

I flung my locker door open—and almost passed out from the stench.

I reeled back, snorting and coughing.

Somewhere behind me, someone began to laugh.

I leaned forward, holding my breath, and peered cautiously into my locker. It was stuffed with magazine pages, the ones with those perfume ads the have really disgusting, stinky perfume in them.

It was intense. And it was probably going to take me for ever to get the scent out of my books, my notebooks, my extra sweatshirt. . .

I turned.

Cary raised his hand in a salute.

What could I do? I returned the salute and then turned my back on him.

I peered into the locker again and began, gingerly, to remove books. And I decided that the first thing I was going to do was buy a new lock. A big, conspicuous one that Cary wouldn't be able to resist trying to open.

And then I was going to rig my locker with the monster of all booby traps. . .

Look out for Mystery No 26

DAWN SCHAFER,
UNDERCOVER BABYSITTER

"How does the puzzle work?" asked Richard, leaning forward. He seemed to have forgotten all about making it home in time for supper.

"When we gathered for the reading of the will, I handed each daughter a sealed envelope," Miss Iorio explained, sounding mysterious. "Inside each envelope was a different clue. There was also an envelope for me, which is to remain sealed until one of the daughters thinks she has solved the puzzle. Inside my envelope is a code, which supposedly will allow me to confirm whether or not the daughter has found the right object."

"Complicated!" Richard remarked.

Miss Iorio nodded. "And sort of silly, really," she continued. "But there's not a thing I can do about it. The executor's job is to carry out the wishes of the deceased, nothing more and nothing less."

"It does seem silly," I mused. "I mean, if the sisters could work together—"

"Exactly!" Miss Iorio cried, interrupting. "That's exactly what I think. If they teamed up, they could use all three clues, work together to find the object and share the inheritance. Right now, though, they're all too selfish to want to share." She smiled at me. "I'll tell you, you baby-sitters ought to try to help them out. I mean, if Justine and Sally would only pull together and hire one sitter—like you!— for all their kids, maybe you could help end the feud."

The

BABYSITTERS Club

Need a babysitter? Then call the Babysitters Club. Kristy Thomas and her friends are all experienced sitters. They can tackle any job from rampaging toddlers to a pandemonium of pets. To find out all about them, read on!

The **CAFÉ** Club

Make room for a delicious helping of the Café Club and meet the members; Fen, Leah, Luce, Jaimini, Tash and Andy. Work has never been so much fun!

1: GO FOR IT, FEN!
Fen and her friends are fed up with being poor. Then Fen has a *brilliant* idea – she'll get them all jobs in her aunt's café! Surely parents and homework won't get in the way of the Café Club...

2: LEAH DISCOVERS BOYS
Leah's got plenty to occupy her – there's the Café Club, homework and the Music Festival. She certainly hasn't got time for boyfriends... But when her music teacher starts picking on her, help arrives in the form of a surprisingly attractive *boy*...

3: LUCE AND THE WEIRD KID
Nothing's working out for Luce at the moment. Grounded ... with *purple* hair ... and now this weird kid's got her into deep trouble at the café...

4: JAIMINI AND THE WEB OF LIES

Sometimes Jaimini wishes she weren't so clever. Then her parents wouldn't want to *ruin* her life by sending her to a posh school away from her friends. But as the Café Club plot to save her, Jaimini meets Dom and begins to change her mind...

5: ANDY THE PRISONER

Andy's parents have gone away and forced her to stay with creaky old Grandma Sorrell ... and forbid her to work in the café! Andy's got to break out - and she knows *just* the friends to help her...

6: TASH'S SECRETS

Tash has a secret wish. She dreams of having a father again. So the Café Club set out to make her dreams come true... But Tash also has another secret *no one* must find out. Because if they do Tash is afraid she will lose her friends...

7: FEN'S REVENGE

Fen's having trouble with boys. Playing stupid, annoying pranks is one thing, but sabotaging an important cross-country race is going too far. Fen's out for revenge ... and the Café Club are right behind her.

Reader beware – here's THREE TIMES
the scare!

Look out for these bumper GOOSEBUMPS
editions. With three spine-tingling stories by
R.L. Stine in each book, get ready for three
times the thrill ... three times the scare ...
three times the GOOSEBUMPS!

GOOSEBUMPS COLLECTION 1
Welcome to Dead House
Say Cheese and Die
Stay Out of the Basement

GOOSEBUMPS COLLECTION 2
The Curse of the Mummy's Tomb
Let's Get Invisible!
Night of the Living Dummy

GOOSEBUMPS COLLECTION 3
The Girl Who Cried Monster
Welcome to Camp Nightmare
The Ghost Next Door

GOOSEBUMPS COLLECTION 4
The Haunted Mask
Piano Lessons Can Be Murder
Be Careful What You Wish For